The *Perfect* Plan

This is a work of fiction. All the characters, organizations, and events portrayed in this novel are products of the author's imagination or used fictitiously.

THE PERFECT PLAN. Copyright © 2020 by Anita Lemke. All rights reserved.

Imprint by Snow Drop Press, LLC.

No parts of this book may be reproduced, scanned, or distributed in any printed or electronic form without permission.

www.anitalemkeauthor.com
Cover design by Melinda de Ross
ISBN 978-1-7350935-2-9

The Perfect Series

The Perfect Match
(Imperfectly Perfect)
The Perfect Plan
The Perfect Bet
The Perfect Lie

Imperfectly *Perfect*

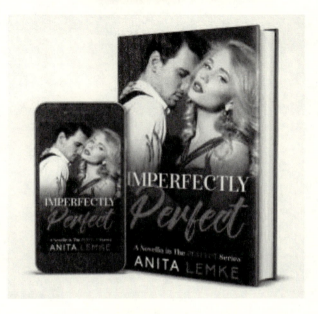

Daughters of wealthy parents don't get to pick their husbands... unless they do.

Download your free book here:
https://anitalemkeauthor.com/imperfectly-perfect/

The Perfect Plan

Book Two in The *Perfect* Series

Chapter 1

HER WEDDING DAY should have been the happiest day of her life. Tonya Corley wore in an elaborate white wedding dress complete with a veil and five-inch heels, which made the appropriate clicking noises when she walked. Her stylist had done a superb job of braiding several small strands of her light blond hair and somehow pinning it together to make her look like a fairy-tale princess. A quick glance in the mirror revealed she had never looked better, even though it was no longer important.

She was not getting married today, or maybe ever.

Before she could move on with the rest of her life, she had to get rid of the wedding party still waiting for her inside the chapel. They already knew what happened. Mark Dunham, the groom—or rather the man who should have been the groom—told them the wedding was off.

What exactly he had told them, she didn't know. Nor did she care. She had no desire to see him ever again. The entire idea had been stupid, anyway.

Tonya would have liked to blame her friend, Victoria, but in all fairness, Victoria had tried to talk her out of it several times. In hindsight, Tonya realized Victoria had followed her own agenda.

Tonya sighed and delicately picked up her dress before she got up. Wearing a wedding dress was glamorous, but only if you actually got married in it.

She would have liked to change into something more appropriate now—maybe sweatpants. Naturally, she hadn't brought a change of clothes. As the bride, it shouldn't have been an issue.

She walked to the big brass door and pushed it open into the main part of the chapel, beautifully decorated for the occasion. There were flowers everywhere. Someone had even placed lacy cushions on the uncomfortable benches. The church itself was quaint, with a traditional altar and stained-glass windows.

Instantly, two dozen pairs of eyes focused on Tonya. She was glad they had planned a small wedding. She couldn't imagine delivering her message to hundreds of people.

Tonya's mother came forward and grabbed her hands. "Is it true there will not be a wedding?"

"Yes, Mom. The wedding is off."

There was an audible gasp from a few members of the group. Tonya wasn't sure if people were genuinely shocked or if her cousins were just having fun. Some of her family members had a flair for drama Tonya didn't share.

It didn't matter. She just needed to clarify one thing.

"What did Mark say?" The last thing she wanted was to contradict whatever story he fed them.

"Mark said it was all his fault. He said he was in love with someone else." Tonya's mother broke off and looked at her daughter. "Did you know about this?"

Tonya sighed. "Not before today."

"But honey, what are we going to do now? You're really not getting married?"

Tonya shook her head almost imperceptibly. Her mother was not helpful. Darlene Corley had old-fashioned ideas. In her mind, all women should get married and have babies, and Tonya was already late to the game.

The *Perfect* Plan

She thought of arguing with her mother, but realized it was pointless. Her mother had been ecstatic when Tonya announced her engagement to Mark. Not only was she finally getting married, but she was also marrying into high society and money. Tonya's wedding would have been the culmination of her mother's dreams.

But it wasn't entirely Tonya's dream. There had been mostly practical considerations.

Tonya was glad Mark had squarely shouldered the blame for her now. She hadn't been innocent in this relationship. Her reasons for getting married hadn't been any nobler than his. And yet, it should have been easy. They had taken love out of the equation and made it a business arrangement.

As she stared out the window for a moment, she remembered how Mark had fit the bill. He had told her from the beginning he just wanted to get access to his trust fund, which he would get upon marriage or turning thirty-five, still a few years away. Victoria, the matchmaker and Tonya's best friend, was the one who had set them up. But then Mark had fallen in love with Victoria, of all people. The worst part was they had both left it until this very morning to tell Tonya the truth.

And yet, she had doubted own decision as she stepped into her gown, even though she hadn't admitted this to anyone. When Mark showed up at the church to tell her he couldn't go through with the wedding because he loved Victoria, a small part of her had felt relief.

It would be fine, Tonya told herself. She just had to get home, and then she could take off this stupid dress.

"Well, there's nothing more to say. I guess the party's over." Tonya spread out her arms.

Several people came up and hugged her. Tonya suddenly felt deflated. If she didn't leave soon, she would start screaming in frustration in the middle of the church. Everyone was feeling sorry for her. It was unbearable.

Suddenly, Daron stepped up.

Why was Daron still here? As Mark's best friend, he would have played the best man at this wedding. About an hour ago, Tonya would have considered him her friend, too. But she knew breakups, even breakups at the altar, made people apt to declare allegiance to one party over the other.

"Would you like me to take you home?" His kind blue eyes regarded her.

Tonya nodded. It was possibly the nicest thing anyone had said to her all day. Obviously, Daron wasn't the kind of guy to leave a woman stranded, even if his best friend was the culprit.

She said her goodbyes and followed Daron out the backdoor. She hadn't even known there was a backdoor. How convenient. Things were finally going her way. Her family would leave through the front, and she could get home without talking to anyone else. She felt grateful to Daron for rescuing her.

When Tonya stepped out into the blinding sunlight, she slowed down her steps. "Where is your car?" She didn't know if she could really walk anywhere without stumbling over her long train.

Daron instantly understood her predicament. "Let me bring the car around."

"I'll wait right here," she said to his retreating back.

Daron was nice, maybe a little too nice. In fact, he reminded her a little of a dog, too eager to please, probably why he was still single.

She could wait a few more minutes if she had to. Not that she wanted to stand outside in the scorching August heat. Her eyes swept past a billboard advertisement for Rhodes Law Firm. At least she didn't need to hire someone like Mr. Rhodes for her divorce later. It was better to break it up now.

She heard someone whistle and holler at her. She turned around but didn't recognize anyone she knew. A group of people on the opposite sidewalk were waving at her. One person was even taking pictures.

Those would be the only pictures of her in a wedding dress. Just great.

Someone whistled. "Where's your husband? If you're looking for one, I'm available!"

Tonya blushed and looked away. This was embarrassing. Where was Daron?

When he finally drove up, Tonya impatiently opened the passenger door. She was about to get in the car when she felt Daron's hand on her back. "Just a moment, let me move the seat for you."

Tonya stepped aside. Of course, he was right. She wouldn't fit in the car with her enormous dress unless there was more room in the front. But she didn't care if the dress got stuck in the door and torn in half. She already had dreams of burning it, anyway.

She grudgingly got in and let him hand her the train. She kicked off her shoes and leaned back while Daron shut the door and walked around to the driver's side.

"I'm not buckling. I can't even see the seat belt," Tonya said defiantly.

He chuckled.

She glared at him.

"I'm sorry," he said. "I know this is not your best day. I'll take you home now, I promise."

"Thanks."

They drove in silence for a while. Tonya replayed the morning in her head. What had gone wrong? It had been such a great idea to get married for practical reasons. She couldn't get her heart broken, because she wasn't in love with Mark. She liked him well enough. He was handsome, soon to be rich, and he had a famous father.

It turned out a guy could still humiliate her before her friends and family, even if she didn't love him. Tonya sighed. Her life was now officially a complete mess.

"Can I ask you something, Tonya?"

"Sure," she said wearily.

"Why did you agree to marry Mark?"

A loaded question. Daron must have known the truth, but maybe he just wanted to hear it from her. Tonya contemplated giving him a flippant answer. Then she decided against it. After his offer to drive her home, she definitely considered him to be her friend. Otherwise, she would have had to ride with her parents, and she couldn't deal with her mother right now.

"I want to go to law school. Mark was going to pay for my studies." It was a little simplistic but explained her situation in a nutshell.

Daron frowned. "If you wanted to go to law school that badly, why didn't you just get student loans?"

Tonya sighed, annoyed they were still on the subject. "My credit got wrecked by my ex-boyfriend."

"It still seems over the top. Getting married to get a degree."

He wasn't wrong.

She explained, "It's not just about the degree. It's a long story."

Tonya's thoughts drifted to her aunt, wondering where she was hiding. She could say a lot more on the subject, but she wasn't about to confide in Daron.

"Thanks for the ride," she said as he pulled into the parking lot of her apartment complex.

"No problem," Daron said. "Hey, let me give you my number in case you need anything."

She looked at him incredulously. Did her wedding dress look like it had pockets for a phone or pen and paper?

"What's your number?" he asked, undaunted. "I just want to call and check in on you."

He didn't give up easily. She had to give him that. She rattled off her phone number and hastily opened the car door.

Daron had to help her again by holding her train and shoes while she awkwardly got out of the car. Apparently, there was no way to do this gracefully when wearing a wedding dress with a giant train.

She took the fabric from him, balled up as it was, and her shoes, and walked up the stairs to her apartment barefoot.

He seemed unsure of what to do. "Can I help you? Do you have a key?"

"I'm fine," Tonya called back.

It had seemed like a great idea to have Daron drive her home, but not if he never left. She might as well have gotten a ride with her mother instead.

Tonya shuddered at the thought of having her mother fuss over her as she dug under the doormat for her key.

There would be no honeymoon for her. Not now. Probably never, at the rate things were going. She closed the door behind her without making sure Daron had left. He would get the hint.

Tonya dropped the shoes in the hallway and walked to her bedroom.

First things first. The dress had to come off. She couldn't get out of it fast enough. In front of the bathroom mirror, she looked at herself critically.

She had just turned thirty, but most people guessed her to be younger. Her face had more lines than when she was in her twenties, but overall, she had few complaints. She had bright blue eyes, a small nose, and full lips. After she removed the pins, her light blond hair fell down to her chest. Its length was the reason she never wore it down, although she would have made a cute Rapunzel. She had the looks and the figure for it, too. She was tall and thin, and as her friends would say, anything looked good on her.

Yet here she was, still single.

Falling in love hadn't worked out for her. Marrying for convenience and money was a bust, too. Maybe it was time to accept her single status as the new normal.

It was time to change her life. From now on, she was done with men. The only thing that mattered was finally getting into law school, however she could make it happen.

***

A weekend of moping was enough. On Monday, Tonya decided it was time to put the pieces of her life back together. In anticipation of becoming Mrs. Dunham, she had quit her job. She would have to find a new one, and fast. She had to talk to the school about her enrollment this fall semester, which was only a couple of weeks away.

She scrolled through her Facebook feed while she listened to hold music. Victoria shared a picture of newlyweds Sylvia and Brandon, a couple she had unwittingly introduced to each other. It reminded Tonya there would probably be a similar picture of Victoria and Mark on social media soon. Her mouse hovered over the unfriend button for a moment. That would be pathetic, Tonya decided. Not unwarranted, but still pathetic. She went back to her feed.

She hummed to the music but halted when Facebook served her with a blast from the past. There was her aunt, laughing into the camera. Tonya's mother was in the picture, too. It was a family barbecue, and Tonya herself could have been just on the other side of the photographer. She sighed as she wondered where her aunt was now. Tonya hoped she was okay.

The voice on the phone broke through her thoughts, and Tonya stuttered as she tried to remember who she was calling and why.

"Thank you for holding, Miss Corley. How can I help you?"

"Is my acceptance still valid if I postpone enrolling for a while?"

"Absolutely. We'll hold your spot for up to a year, at the most. You must come and sign some papers. As long as you enroll by fall next year, you won't have to start over with the application process."

"That's great. I'll be by later to sign the papers. I appreciate your," Tonya said.

Tonya carefully laid the phone on the table and took a deep breath. She could scream and cry all she wanted to, but it wouldn't help. Law school was out, for now.

Marrying Mark would have solved all her problems. Instead, she would have to scramble to find an income source to keep the electricity turned on since she had quit her job in anticipation of becoming Mrs. Dunham.

Time for Plan B... she needed a high-paying job. A quick Internet search revealed only one open position in her chosen career field within a thirty-mile radius. It wasn't the *only* job in the city of Radfield. If she would scrub toilets, she wouldn't starve. But those jobs wouldn't pay her tuition for law school. She read the ad.

Wanted: Paralegal for new law office. Some overtime necessary. Great starting salary. Call Patrick Rhodes for more information.

Rhodes. He was the guy on the billboard.

Maybe this was her chance. She looked up the address online. The property was in The Meadows. Everyone who was anyone lived in The Meadows. It was a subdivision full of multi-million-dollar homes. Tonya whistled softly. This lawyer would attract clientele with deep pockets.

The name was equally impressive... *Patrick Rhodes*.

Rhodes. They were a prominent family in Radfield. His name alone would help him succeed.

She copied the address and set her alarm. Instead of calling ahead for more information, she would stand on the lawyer's doorstep first thing in the morning.

***

As Tonya drove through Radfield in the morning, she went over the job description in her head. What could the lawyer gain by hiring her?

She drove through the small Texas town without paying attention to the familiar surroundings. Radfield prided itself on having the most vibrant downtown area in any small town in Texas, and the city officials weren't wrong. Instead of having rows of deserted shops around the square—a common site all over the country—Radfield's little community was thriving.

As she reached The Willows, she hummed to herself. This was a nice place to live with mature trees, enormous yards, and beautiful houses. On second thought, maybe these houses were better described as mansions. It didn't take long until she found the right one.

She parked the car and peeked at the house before she checked her outfit for flaws. Her gray pencil skirt and white blouse were spotless. Tonya double-checked her makeup in the rearview mirror. She definitely looked the part. She was smart enough to do paralegal work, too, even though she didn't have a paralegal certification. She had been a legal secretary at her last job, and the only reason she hadn't done paralegal work was a lack of opportunity. At home, she routinely poured over law books, constantly adding to her collection by purchasing used textbooks from the local university.

She only needed to convince this lawyer to give her a chance.

When she got out of the car, she noticed how quiet it was. The only noise was the clicking of her shoes on the pavement. Was it too early to show up? She squared her shoulders. There was only one way to find out.

Tonya rang the doorbell and stepped back to admire the house. It was a sprawling building on a half-acre lot. As much as she wanted to dismiss the house as an extravagantly rich person's fancy, it had character. Tonya's eyes traveled over the red-brick exterior, the brown shutters next to each of the windows, and an inviting front door. She was just wondering if she could look in through the stained glass from the outside when the door opened and a man in his early thirties stepped out to greet her.

He didn't even look like a lawyer, especially not the Mr. Rhodes she had seen on the billboard. That lawyer had looked slick, while this guy was wearing jeans and a T-shirt. His dark hair was rumpled, but what she could see of his arms showed signs of an active gym membership. He could be the gardener, except his clothes were spotless. He was at least six feet tall as she had to look up to meet his eyes, which were a startling blue.

"I'm here for Patrick Rhodes. Am I at the right place?"

"Depends. What do you want?"

A typical non-answer only politicians and lawyers would give. But now was not the time to get worked up over etiquette. She was here to get a job.

She smiled politely and extended her hand. "I'm Tonya Corley and would like to speak to you about the paralegal position."

He frowned and rubbed his stubbly chin.

Tonya looked at the number on the house. Was she at the wrong place? A quick glance at her paperwork confirmed the address again. Why did this guy look annoyed to see an applicant?

"You placed an ad in the Radfield Gazette?" Tonya slowly lowered her hand when it became obvious he wouldn't shake it. What a weird guy.

"Yes, I did," he said slowly, as if he wished the opposite was true.

"Am I too late? Have you filled the position?"

"Not exactly," he said as he looked at her with displeasure. His ocean-blue eyes were assessing her carefully.

He had no interest in hiring her. She did not understand what had put him off. Was it her outfit? She almost turned around and walked away, but anger stopped her. He hadn't even given her a proper chance.

She boldly handed him a copy of her resume, which he took reluctantly. "I can start right away. I work hard and I get things done."

"Look, I've changed my mind. I'm not hiring," he said.

Tonya looked at him in disbelief. He was pulling her leg, wasn't he? He was about to shut the door in her face when Tonya wedged her foot in, "Wait!"

Patrick Rhodes slowly opened the door again, exasperation obvious in his features.

"I *will* notice when a new employee starts here tomorrow or next week. I'm sure you're an equal opportunity employer."

"Of course I am." He sounded annoyed.

They both knew any other answer would not have been legal. She had won this first battle, and she couldn't help smiling triumphantly as he gestured for her to come in.

Once inside, she gasped at her surroundings. He hadn't purchased a single piece of furniture in this room at a modern store. Everything was antique or specially made for this house, from the cuckoo clock in the corner to the giant grandfather's desk in the reception area. The cream-colored couch along the wall looked too valuable to touch, let alone sit on. Above it, Tonya noticed a picture of Patrick, the Mr. Rhodes from the billboard, a woman similar to him in age, and an elderly gentleman. She didn't dwell on it, but the family resemblance was obvious.

The only modern things in the room were the computer and printer on the desk and a dozen assorted cables.

His eyes followed her gaze toward the desk and he said, "I've been fighting with this stuff all morning. I was trying to network the printer with the computers."

She nodded slowly as an idea occurred to her. Here was her chance to prove herself. She put her purse on the chair and examined the cables.

"I'll fix it for you," she said.

"You don't have to do that."

"I'm happy to help. Ask me anything while I work on this. It shouldn't take more than five minutes."

He watched her with uncertainty. Tonya wasn't sure if he was glad she was helping or still annoyed she was here at all.

"Alright. Well, thanks, I guess," he said. "What other experience would you bring to this job?"

She glanced at him before sorting through the cables. "As far as job experience goes, I've worked as a legal secretary for five years. I write up letters, handle the scheduling, and meet the clients."

It was one thing she had going for her. Her employment history was solid, even though she had never worked as a paralegal before.

"Hmm."

"Would you please pull on this cable?" She was under the desk now, trying hard to prevent her skirt from hiking up while pushing a cable through a hole at the top of the desk.

He grabbed the cable and held it until she surfaced again, smoothing out her outfit. Some of her hair had come out of her ponytail, and she brushed it away from her face as she took the cable from his hands, careful not to touch him directly.

"You haven't really done any paralegal work then? Writing up contracts or helping with depositions?"

"No. But I'm an avid student of the law. I read anything I can get my hands on. All I need is an opportunity to show what I can do."

He nodded, thoughtfully.

She turned on the computer and sat down. There was no password to get in, and she chose not to tell him how careless he was being.

"There you go," she said, handing him the test page she had just printed.

He smiled. "Outstanding. Thanks."

"Anytime." She returned his smile and noticed for the first time how handsome he was. She glanced at his hand. No ring. How was a lawyer this attractive still unmarried?

"Look, I can see you're smart and motivated. But I really need to hire someone with experience. I can't afford to hire a paralegal and a secretary," he said. "I need to start small and grow from there. Maybe I can offer you a job in the future, but this position isn't the right fit for you."

Suddenly, his blue eyes seemed cold and distant.

"What if I worked here on a trial basis?" She had to give it another try, although she felt pathetic for asking.

"I don't think so."

"Well. Thanks, anyway," she said.

She would not try to shake hands with him again. She would just make a graceful exit. She looked around for her purse.

"Look, it's not you. I was just looking to hire someone... different."

He seemed to notice her furtive glance and held her purse out to her. She took it without a word of thanks. She had to force herself not to slam the door as she left the house.

What a nutcase.

On the way home, her thoughts were running wild. She had been sure this job was for her. It was really her only option if she wanted to earn decent money. There wasn't much else in Radfield for paralegals or secretaries. And she speculated there couldn't be many people applying for this job, either, but Patrick Rhodes hadn't wanted to hire her.

He would have shown her the door if she hadn't literally wedged her way in. But why?

There must be something she could do. Maybe her friend Victoria could pull some strings for her. Victoria wined and dined Radfield's finest citizens and probably knew someone who could help.

But Tonya dismissed the idea as quickly as she thought of it. She wasn't ready to talk to Victoria. She needed to get this job on her own. Victoria's "help" had landed her where she was in the first place, unmarried and jobless.

Back home, Tonya parked the car, grabbed her mail, and took the stairs up to her apartment two steps at a time. As she walked in, she flipped through the envelopes. Three bills and a collection notice. She cringed as she carefully put them on her kitchen table and sat down. She pulled out her laptop and started a new job search before she had even taken off her shoes.

The only jobs she could find were minimum-wage or entry-level jobs. Waitress. Cashier. Sales Associate. There were a few openings in the medical field she didn't qualify for. Dental Hygienist. Nurse.

She closed her eyes briefly. She could always find a way to pay the bills, but law school would stay out of reach unless she got a job with the lawyer. She glanced at the collection notice and frowned.

Maybe there was a way she could get hired. She just needed some leverage.

Tonya typed Rhodes Law Firm into the browser's search bar. She found the website for Patrick Rhodes and started reading. Maybe she could figure out what he needed most in a paralegal. If that didn't work, maybe she could find the chink in his armor and worm her way in.

On a whim, Tonya checked his license to practice law—all good. Another search of his name revealed nothing interesting besides his law school yearbook picture and a link to a silly video.

But then she suddenly remembered the house. The Meadows was a residential area, and an expensive one. And he planned to practice law out of his stately home. Why else would he hook up the computers downstairs and make it look like an office?

"That's it."

Her fingers flew over the keyboard. In less than two minutes, she had her answer in black and white.

The city of Radfield didn't allow anyone to use their home as a business inside of city limits. Zoning laws weren't this strict everywhere in Texas, but Radfield had many prominent—read "rich"—citizens who wanted to protect their privacy.

She printed the document and read it word for word. There was no mistaking it. The lawyer clearly violated zoning laws.

For a moment, she struggled with her conscience. Could she worm her way into this job by blackmailing him about the zoning laws? She glanced at the collection notice beside her. What choice did she have?

And it wasn't as if hiring her would be a hardship for him. She was good at her job, and she was really doing him a favor.

The local zoning laws would be her secret weapon. She would go back to the lawyer and convince him to hire her.

"You haven't seen the last of me, Patrick Rhodes," Tonya mumbled to herself.

There was hope. Just as she shut down the computer, she heard the doorbell ring.

Chapter 2

NOBODY LIKED TO SHOW UP unannounced as often as Tonya's mother. Tonya had tried to explain to her social protocol dictated she call beforehand, but her words always fell on deaf ears. Her mother would do as she pleased, and Tonya tried to tolerate it as best as she could.

"I brought you some muffins, dear."

"Thank you." There was no sense in telling her mother muffins had too many carbs.

Darlene Corley was about five foot five, slightly shorter than her daughter. It was easy to see she enjoyed cooking and baking for her family because her shirts always had flour on them. Darlene herself ate like a bird; she gave most of the goodies away as gifts. And unlike the typical cheery countenance of a baker, Tonya's mom was slender with graying hair and a permanent frown, as if worry was her only companion.

Tonya placed the muffins on the kitchen counter when she remembered the bills on the table. Maybe the kitchen was not a good place to hang out. Tonya grabbed the muffins and gently guided her mother into the living room. Before they sat down, Tonya collected several piles of paper from the sofa and put them in a stack in the corner of the room. Darlene Corley rolled her eyes but refrained from commenting on the mess.

Instead, she seemed to goad her by saying, "It's such a shame you live here all by yourself."

Tonya suppressed a laugh. "I'm fine, Mom."

"You need a husband to give you some purpose. And children to look after. You're not getting any younger."

Tonya rolled her eyes. "There's more to life than getting married, Mom."

"Sure there is." Darlene surveyed her daughter as if she was trying to figure out where to place her in the marriage market. "Didn't Lindy Faulkner's boy drive you home the other day?"

Tonya flinched. "You mean Daron?"

"Yes, that's his name. He's a nice sort."

"How do you know Daron, Mom?"

"Lindy and I have been friends for a long time. She raised him practically by herself. She's still got her hands full with her daughter, too."

Tonya shrugged her shoulders. Daron's background didn't interest her in the least.

"Daron Faulkner is a nice boy." Her mother sighed.

"Yes, he's very nice, just like Mark. I'm not interested in Daron."

Tonya got up from her chair and paced around the room. It annoyed her that her mother came over unannounced, but she hated it even more when her mother told her how to live her life. She probably imagined a wedding between her and Daron, despite the fiasco of her recent attempt to get married.

"In case you've already forgotten, I tried getting married. And it didn't work out."

"There are other fish in the sea, Tonya."

"I don't want to get married right now. I would much rather travel. I want to see the Acropolis and the Parthenon."

Tonya caught the blank look on her mother's face.

The *Perfect* Plan

"Athens, Greece. I want to go to Greece," Tonya said impatiently.

"Oh. I know. You've been talking about that since you were twelve and you read the weird book about the horse."

"The Trojan Horse."

"Yeah, that one. But how are you going to travel without a husband to pay for it?" Darlene Corley took one of her muffins and picked a crumb off of it. "And didn't you want to go to school again? Weren't you going to start in the fall?"

"I do. I still want to go to law school, but I deferred my enrollment until I figure out how to pay for it."

"You don't have to become a lawyer to help women like your aunt."

Tonya sank onto the couch, surprised at her mother's comment.

It had been a long time since they had talked about her aunt Allyson. Allyson was Darlene's older sister, who never got along with her parents and married as soon as she turned eighteen. The first few years of her marriage seemed blissful, although Allyson rarely visited her family. Sadly, nobody thought anything of it since there had been so much conflict beforehand.

But then Allyson stopped coming to family gatherings altogether. At some point, an observant neighbor noticed bruises on her arms and contacted another family member.

When Tonya was little, Aunt Allyson would tell her outrageous bedtime stories. Tonya remembered vivid tales of gingerbread men, teddy bears, and cherished dolls setting out on big adventures. Aunt Allyson's eyes would sparkle with joy when Tonya giggled and begged for another story.

Years later, however, there was no joy in Aunt Allyson's eyes. It was as if the light had gone out and nobody was even home anymore. Tonya would beg her to tell a story, but Aunt Allyson would just shake her head sadly.

Much later, Tonya learned more about what had happened. At some point, Allyson tried to leave her abusive husband and filed for a divorce, but she couldn't afford to pay for a lawyer since her husband handled the money.

Aunt Allyson found a women's shelter and hid. As far as Tonya knew, she never worked up the courage to file for divorce again and was still hiding somewhere, moving from place to place but always returning to Radfield or its surrounding countryside. And yet, Aunt Allyson never contacted her own family, presumably for fear of being found.

With this family history, helping women like Aunt Allyson had become an obsession for Tonya. Maybe it was too late to help her aunt, but she could help other women in similar situations.

Tonya already volunteered at the local safe house for women every week, helping them with their paperwork. But if she had a law degree, she knew she could do more. She could represent them in court and protect them from further violence.

"You don't speak Greek, do you?" Her mother deftly changed the subject and brought Tonya out of her reverie.

Aunt Allyson wasn't a topic her mom liked to dwell on. Tonya assumed it stirred up too many unwanted emotions for her.

"No, but it's not important, Mom. It's just a dream. Not all dreams come true."

"Getting married and having babies is a different dream."

Tonya shook her head. She might never understand her mother, but she knew where her idea of women's roles came from. Tonya's grandparents were staunch believers in marrying for practical purposes. Tonya's mother probably felt lucky for having found a man who treated her well enough. It was easy to see why she still considered it to be a man's world, where a woman needed the protection of a good husband.

"I'm just saying. You're an only child, and I want grandchildren," Tonya's mother wheedled.

There was probably some truth in that. Her mother had a lot of free time on her hands, and grandchildren would give her something to do besides baking high-calorie desserts. Tonya smiled, leaned over, and kissed her mother on the cheek. Her mother would always want things she couldn't give to her.

"How is Daddy doing?"

"He's fine, grumpy as always. He sends his love."

Tonya nodded. She had never understood her parent's relationship. They were committed to sticking it out together, but she couldn't picture them being in love. When she asked her mother about it a long time ago, her mother shrugged it off. Being married wasn't about being in love, Tonya had learned from her. It was about hard work and commitment.

Tonya's parents had never had enough money, either.

Tonya wanted to do things differently. She had always pictured herself falling in love with someone and getting her very own happy-ever-after. Before the debacle with Mark, she was head-over-heels-in-love and had dreamed of marrying Nick. When the relationship fell apart, she decided she would at least marry someone wealthy enough to pay for law school. But neither of those plans had worked.

Still, marrying without love or money made no sense.

Tonya grabbed a muffin and bit into it. "This is good, Mom."

And she meant it. Her mother's baking was heavenly. Tonya eyed the half-eaten muffin on her mother's plate. She would never have the willpower to eat just a bite of one.

Her cell phone rang as she swallowed the last crumb, and she glanced at the display. Another call from a collection agency. She silenced her phone as she faced her mother, who was staring at her intensely.

"Is everything alright?"

"Yes," Tonya lied, trying to push her financial worries out of her mind. Her eyes drifted to the clock. She needed to get back to Patrick Rhodes' house before it was too late. "Listen, Mom, I have a little errand to run."

"I'll come with you."

Tonya imagined the horror of her mother going job-hunting with her. Her mother didn't even know she was out of a job. For another, she was about to blackmail her way into getting hired. Not her proudest moment.

"Well, actually, I don't think that's such a good idea," Tonya said, hesitation in her voice.

Her mother sighed. "Have it your way. I'll go home, but I'm leaving the muffins."

Tonya almost objected, but realized it was futile. Better to get her mother out of here now and worry about the carbs later.

Since she didn't have time to change, but she quickly braided her hair to keep it in place this time. Not that she had any plans to do any more pro bono work for this guy. If he didn't hire her, he could connect his stupid computers and printers alone.

She found the house again with ease and got out of her car. This time, she didn't admire the building before she rang the doorbell. Her heart hammered in her chest as she clutched the printout in her hand. Would he even open the door when he saw her standing there?

Apparently, he wasn't one to shy away from confrontations because the door opened right away. And there he was, frowning at her again. He had shaved and showered and put on different clothes since this morning—slacks and a Polo shirt, which emphasized his biceps. His hair still looked disheveled, as if he hadn't cared enough to style it.

His voice was gruff. "Why are you here again?"

So much for saying hello.

Tonya wordlessly handed him the paper she had printed. He glared at her but perused it silently. As soon as he realized what he was reading, he looked at her. If looks could kill, she would have been dead and buried.

"What does this have to do with anything?"

"You're in obvious violation of local zoning laws," Tonya said with a sweet-as-honey voice.

"I can read."

"I have a feeling the city of Radfield would love to know this about you."

He cursed under his breath.

She had to suppress a grin. She got his attention. Now the trick was to keep it and use it to her advantage.

"Your neighbors might also be interested to learn you're planning to practice law from your home," she added.

He shot her another look that would have frightened anyone away, but she wasn't ready to give up.

"Why don't we talk about this inside?" She smiled innocently.

He gave her a dirty look but opened the door just enough for her to slip by. She didn't flinch when he shut it behind him with a bang.

"What do you want from me?" He threw the now crumpled paper on the floor.

"I want you to hire me. I'm great at what I do. I know the law. I'm great with clients and printers. Give me a chance."

"I'm not hiring just any woman who shows up at my door for this job."

Her eyebrows rose, and she said carefully, "I'm not just *any woman*."

"You're not qualified. You have zero experience."

At least he had read her resume.

"And you're not allowed to practice law here," she retorted.

"I'm renting a location in town. It's just going to take another couple of months to sort out the lease. These are temporary offices." He crossed his arms in front of his chest. "Nobody cares about zoning laws."

"I'm sure the city of Radfield would disagree with you."

"Are you blackmailing me?"

"Of course not. It would be against the law as is discrimination based on gender, race, and ethnicity."

He groaned.

Tonya took a deep breath. Bickering with this guy would not help her.

"Look," she said, lowering her voice in an effort to be conciliatory. "This is not a hardship for you. I'm doing you a favor. Hire me, and I'll prove it to you."

She stared at him, and he returned her gaze unblinkingly. It felt silly, but she had the feeling the staring contest would make or break her case. Fortunately, he turned his eyes away first.

She waited. It was his turn to say something. There was nothing else she could say or do. She had laid her cards on the table.

He started pacing the room, presumably thinking of ways to outwit her. Suddenly, he turned around and faced her. "You don't give up easily, do you?"

Tonya smiled uncertainly in response.

"Not a terrible quality in an employee." He looked at her with sudden determination. "I'll hire you, under one condition."

She forced herself to remain silent and keep a straight face, even though she felt like screaming and jumping up and down with joy.

"Which condition?"

"You must obey the rules. We'll go over them tomorrow. They're not negotiable."

She hesitated. "What rules?"

"Nothing difficult."

She nodded. Fair enough. She was sure she could handle any of his silly rules.

"And two..."

"You said one condition."

The *Perfect* Plan

"Now there are two." He glared at her. "Keep your mouth shut about the zoning."

She tried not to grin. This would be her hold on him until he moved offices. By then, she would have proved her worth as an employee. She was sure of it.

"I want part of the profits."

"What?"

"Profit sharing. I help you with your cases, and you share the profits with me," she said.

"That's ridiculous."

"So is discriminating based on gender."

"I never said I wouldn't hire you because you're a woman. I can't believe this," he said.

"I can read between the lines. But we can agree on a bonus structure tomorrow," she said.

He shook his head as if he was hoping it would make her disappear.

She held out her hand. "Deal?"

"I don't do handshakes."

She frowned. Maybe he was a germaphobe. Verbal contracts sealed with a handshake weren't easy to enforce.

"No problem. Let's sign a contract," she said.

"Tomorrow morning. Be here at eight a.m. sharp."

There was no point in pressing the matter further. She had done what she had set out to do. Tonya smiled sweetly. "See you at eight."

Then she turned around and walked confidently to the door. This time, she felt like whistling and singing. She waited with both until she was in the car driving home for fear he would change his mind.

The job was hers.

***

By the time the sun finally rose in the sky the next morning, Tonya had already spent two hours cleaning the kitchen and prepping dinner at the local women's shelter. The large rumbling farmhouse currently housed eighteen women and their children. While the residents often helped in the kitchen, some of them never left their rooms. It took every counselor the shelter could afford to help these women get a new lease on life. The job included helping them with legal paperwork, but it also entailed household chores like she was doing now. After a quick look at her watch, Tonya hurriedly cleaned the cutting board and loaded the dishwasher.

Before she could sneak out unnoticed, Sabrina greeted her on the stairs with a shy smile.

"Hi Tonya, thanks for helping," she said.

Tonya smiled in return. Sabrina, their newest resident, always had a kind word for everyone.

"I was wondering, if it's not too much trouble, could we talk sometime? Sally said you helped her with her divorce paperwork and found a lawyer for her."

"Of course," Tonya said.

She had referred Sally to her old law office, and they had taken her on as a pro bono case. She had no idea if her new lawyer did pro bono work. She would just have to talk him into it.

"I'll be back later this week. I'll bring some forms, and we'll go over your case, okay?"

Sabrina smiled. "Do you think I could get child support?"

"I hope so, but we'll get it all figured out. I promise," Tonya said.

On her drive home, Tonya wondered how she would convince her new employer to take on a pro bono case. Worst-case scenario, she planned to help Sabrina even if it meant doing the work herself and finding another lawyer who signed off on the case. If only she had a law degree already, it wouldn't even be an issue.

As Tonya raced up the stairs to her apartment to change, her phone rang. It was Victoria calling her for the hundredth time since her canceled wedding day less than a week ago. She missed having Victoria in her life.

The *Perfect* Plan

Could she really blame her for falling in love, even if it was with the man she had planned to marry?

Tonya glanced at the clock. She had ten minutes to get ready. If the conversation went sour, she could legitimately cut it short.

Tonya picked up the phone as she opened the door.

"Hi Tonya." Victoria's voice on the other line sounded relieved and guilty at the same time. "How have you been?"

Tonya thought about giving a flippant response, but then decided against it. This was Victoria, her best friend. And if she was honest with herself, Tonya was excited to hear from her.

"Pretty good, actually. About to start a new job. How are you?"

"Good. Wow, a new job? That's wonderful news, especially considering how much you hated your old job."

Tonya put Victoria on speaker and set the phone on the dresser. She had enough time to change and have a conversation, but only if she multi-tasked—something she excelled at.

"Well, yeah. I kind of had to find a new job after quitting the other one."

"I'm sorry, Tonya," Victoria said. "I should never have agreed to set you up with Mark. And I should have told you sooner."

"Right. Well, you should have told me sooner, but I'm over it."

"Do you really mean it?" Victoria sounded incredulous.

Tonya sighed as she buttoned her blouse. She had given this a lot of thought in the last week, but it was hard to blame Victoria for falling in love—something which happened involuntarily.

"Look, we both know I was never in love with Mark. It's not like I'm heartbroken. It's just not what I had planned for my life. I want to be happy for you."

"That's big of you," Victoria said. "It means a lot to me."

Tonya slipped into her shoes. "Well, I gotta run. I don't want to be late for my first day. But it was nice talking to you."

"Same here," Victoria said with a smile in her voice.

And it had been nice to talk to Victoria. Maybe they could patch their friendship back together bit by bit.

Right now, she had other things to worry about. After another quick look in the mirror to check her hair, Tonya grabbed her purse and raced down the stairs again. She would not risk being late.

Tonya showed up at her new place of work ten minutes before eight. There was no question Patrick Rhodes wouldn't hesitate one moment before reneging on his promise or firing her outright.

When he opened the door, she inhaled sharply.

He looked fine in black slacks and a light blue, long-sleeve, buttoned shirt. The shirt matched the color of his eyes, which seemed friendlier today. And even though he wasn't wearing a tie, he looked formal. He had even styled his hair.

He let her in without a word or a smile, but she wouldn't let him intimidate her.

"Please have a seat, Miss Corley." He gestured to the couch in the corner, and she carefully sat down. "I printed your employment contract for you to peruse."

She accepted the copy he handed to her and started reading carefully. She smiled at the salary and profit-sharing plan. It was better than she had hoped, but she kept reading without commenting. Most of it was standard, she noted. He had covered office hours, dress code, vacation time, and benefits.

Then she came to a section titled rules. She looked at him uncertainly.

"These rules are not negotiable. I want you to initial next to each of them."

The *Perfect* Plan

"Number one, no first names," she read out loud. She shrugged. Fine with her. She would be Miss Corley, and he would be Mr. Rhodes.

She continued reading aloud, "Number two, there must always be two feet between employee and employer when no witnesses are present."

She looked up at him. Was he serious? What kind of nutcase was he?

He raised his eyebrows, daring her to say something about it.

Surely, he must know how stupid this rule was. She had already violated it twice today. There weren't two feet between them when he opened the door or when he handed her the paper.

"Why two feet?"

"Just a precautionary measure."

She frowned.

"It's like buckling your seatbelt to protect yourself in case of a car crash. It doesn't mean your car will crash when you buckle up," he explained.

Metaphors were not his strength, she decided. And what if he was paranoid? There was no need to get closer than two feet, was there? She decided she would play along. She didn't exactly have any other options.

Patrick Rhodes kept talking, "It's easy to keep this kind of distance. You work at your desk. I'll stay in my office. If you want me to sign something, you can email it to me. If you want to talk to me, call me."

She almost laughed at the ridiculousness of it all, but she sensed he wouldn't appreciate it. He acted much too seriously for her to make jokes. Maybe he would loosen up after a while. Then again, it didn't matter to her. There was no need to be physically close to work together successfully.

For a moment, she wondered if she was doing the right thing. She would work for this guy, who clearly had issues. Then again, she didn't have a lot of options, and this job offered her the paycheck she needed to pay for law school.

She would abide by his rules. Not a big deal.

"Okay." She added her initials.

"Rule number three: clients always come first."

"Makes sense," she said.

"If we have an important case to work on, I expect you to put in extra hours to get the work done. If a client calls, you need to answer the phone, preferably on the first ring. If you're typing up a contract and a client walks in, you need to stop and greet them first. Is that clear?"

She nodded and couldn't help but grin. He said she would type up contracts. She would do real legal work. She felt almost giddy. It was like a dream come true. She returned her attention to the contract and initialed rules five through eight without comment.

"Rule number nine is important, too. As you know, I live in this house. You're welcome to use the bathroom and the facilities on this first floor, but you may not come upstairs. If you need me, call me on the phone. Don't send clients up there, either."

"Yes, sir."

Obviously, she wouldn't go up to his home. What did he take her for?

"I need you to download a W9 and fill it out and send it to the printer. I already set you up with a work email last night."

"Great." She signed the contract with a flourish and was about to hand it back to him when she remembered his silly two-foot rule.

He didn't seem to notice she felt rooted to her spot, afraid to get in his way, afraid to violate the rules she just agreed to. When he walked over to the window, she got up and moved behind her new desk. If he came too close while she was behind this desk, it would not be her fault.

"Questions?"

"Not yet," she said.

"I'll be in my office." He shut the door firmly behind him, and for a moment, she felt completely alone.

When the phone rang a minute later, she froze. What was she supposed to say? It rang a second time before she picked up.

"Good morning, you have reached the law office of Patrick Rhodes, Tonya Corley speaking."

"Your greeting is too long. You're not offering to help anyone. And the phone rang twice," Patrick's deep voice criticized her.

She blushed. He was testing her, and she had failed.

"Law office of Patrick Rhodes. How may I help you?"

"Better." He hung up.

She exhaled. She had taken the first hurdle successfully.

And for the rest of the day, she didn't have time to worry about any of his weird rules. He sent her half a dozen emails with assignments to keep her busy for the rest of the week. The phone rang several times, and Tonya scheduled a handful of appointments for him. It was clear his practice was growing. She could tell he had the drive to make a success of his law firm, and nothing would stand in his way, especially not a paralegal more than two feet away from him.

**

Her first week on the job went by in a flash. By the time Friday rolled around, Tonya was looking forward to the weekend. Patrick Rhodes—or Mr. Rhodes as she always referred to him per his rules—was not an awful boss to work for. He provided coffee, which wasn't as good as a latte macchiato from the local coffee shop, but better than nothing.

And while he never acted overly friendly, he took his time to answer her questions. Over the phone, of course. Whenever she heard his voice on the phone, he seemed like a different person altogether. He was even likeable.

But in person, he was consistently gruff with her. It was frustrating and downright annoying.

On Friday afternoon, an elderly couple walked in. It wasn't clear who was supporting whom. He was using a cane, and she was leaning heavily on him. Tonya jumped up and assisted them to the couch. She provided them with extra cushions and brought them each a cup of coffee.

"How very kind of you, my dear." The woman smiled at her gratefully.

Tonya couldn't help but smile back at them. It touched her heart to see how they literally leaned on each other.

"My name is Tonya Corley. I help Mr. Rhodes with his cases. What can I do for the two of you today?"

"I'm not sure if you can help us at all, but we're in a bit of a pickle." The old lady sighed. "My name is Betty Sheffield, and this is my husband, Harold Sheffield. A few months ago, a seemingly nice young man came to our house and convinced us to invest with his company."

"He told us he would keep our money safe from inflation." Her husband spoke gruffly. "I should have known he was a scoundrel."

"You couldn't have, dear. We had no idea," she added, looking at Tonya. "His eyes were unkind. I was hesitant at first, but then he told me he had signed up several of our neighbors." She shrugged. "Mrs. Duprey is a better judge of character than I am. At least that's what I thought."

Tonya listened in disbelief as the couple finished their story. They had authorized wire transfers to a company called Cobblestone Investments. For several months, the Sheffields had received statements listing their balance, which seemed to grow at a fast rate.

"Ten percent interest every month. It was too good to be true." Mr. Sheffield balled his hand in a fist.

"Anyway, we had a medical emergency come up and needed some money to pay for it." Mrs. Sheffield dabbed her eyes with a tissue. "That's when we found out it was all a hoax. We wrote letters. We called. The letters came back undeliverable, and nobody answered the phone."

"It's despicable is what it is—as if the government didn't already take enough of our money." Mr. Sheffield was getting worked up now.

"Our neighbors are in the same boat. Nobody can get a hold of this company. And our money is gone," Mrs. Sheffield said as she patted her husband on the arm. "It'll be alright, dear."

"How awful," Tonya said.

"So here we are." Mrs. Sheffield spread out her hands.

"If you don't mind me asking, how much money did they take from you?"

"Everything." Mr. Sheffield said. "They took every last penny of our money, those rascals."

Mrs. Sheffield handed Tonya a paper with a number written on it. Tonya's eyes widened in shock.

"Do you have any of the paperwork with you?" Tonya was eager to sink her teeth into this case. She couldn't wait to dig in and find out who was behind the scam.

"Yes, dear. It's still in the car. We didn't know if the lawyer could see us right now." Mrs. Sheffield looked at her questioningly.

"Let me talk to him and see what I can do. And then I'll be happy to get the paperwork out of the car and make copies for our files. Can I get you anything else in the meantime? A glass of water?"

"Thank you, dear. We're fine." Mrs. Sheffield smiled kindly as she shot a concerned look at her husband, who was still muttering to himself.

Tonya walked over to Mr. Rhodes' office. She knocked on the door twice, then opened it and walked in, closing the door behind her.

Patrick Rhodes was reading a thick brief on his desk, making notes along the way. He looked up as she walked in, flustered to see her in his space.

"I'm sorry to interrupt, but there's an elderly couple in the waiting room who needs to see you. A company scammed them out of all their money, and all their neighbors are in the same boat. This could be a big case."

"How much money are we talking about?"

Typical. All he thought about was the money. She was careful to keep her voice neutral. There was no sense in antagonizing her employer at this point.

"Half a million dollars. And that's just their money. Their neighbors all did the same thing. This could be huge."

He emitted a low whistle. "That must be their entire life savings."

Tonya looked at him in surprise. Maybe she had misjudged him. She was glad he appreciated the seriousness of the situation from the client's point of view.

"I'll see them right now. Get me copies of any paperwork they have," he said.

"I'm on it."

After Mr. and Mrs. Sheffield had shuffled into his office, Tonya got to work at the copier. They had a lot of paperwork, even a 60-page contract. Tonya worried about what she would find in there. There was sure to be some language in there, allowing the company to take the couple's money and run. It was hardly legal and still nothing but a scam.

Eventually, Mr. and Mrs. Sheffield left the office. Tonya was glad to see Mr. Rhodes escort them to their car. She followed and returned their folder to them.

"I've made copies of everything in here. If you find anything else, we'll copy it, too."

"Thank you, dear." Mrs. Sheffield shook her hand and got into the passenger seat. Mr. Sheffield ambled around the car and deposited his cane in the backseat.

"See you this evening," Mr. Rhodes called after them.

Tonya looked at him questioningly. He planned to visit a client after hours?

"I'll explain in a minute," he whispered to her.

After they walked back inside, Tonya got behind her desk while he sat on the couch, keeping plenty of distance between them. She looked at him expectantly.

"Do you have any plans tonight?" he asked.

"What?"

"You heard me."

"I don't see how it's any of your business. I don't work in the evenings," Tonya said shortly.

"I'm aware of that. I wrote your employment contract," he said dryly. "But this case with the Sheffields has the potential to be huge. I'm going to their house to talk to them. I may also talk to some of their neighbors, at least get some names. It would be really helpful if you could come along and take notes."

"Are you asking me to work overtime?"

"I'm giving you a chance to work extra hours. You'll get overtime pay. But by law, I can't make you." His tone of voice was barely polite now.

Tonya rolled her eyes at him. "If you just asked me nicely, I'd be happy to help, you know."

He sighed and said, "Will you please come with me tonight, Miss Corley?"

She smiled sweetly. "I would be happy to."

"Great. Let's make a plan."

Judging by the speed with which he moved on, he had clearly not expected her to say no. Did he always get his way?

Patrick Rhodes got up and paced the room while she remained silent. "We need as much information as we can about this guy who came around. We need to know what they've given him. Presumably, they gave him a check. We need to speak to the bank and talk to them about fraudulent withdrawals. We need names, addresses, and phone numbers of the other neighbors involved."

Tonya took notes furiously while he talked. She could feel the adrenaline pumping through her veins. This would be the first big case she was involved in from start to finish.

"I need you to research the legal precedent. Make another copy of the contract, so we can both go through it at the same time. First step is discovering who's behind the scam. If we can't pinpoint the blame on a big company, there's no point in pursuing this case at all. Questions?" Patrick Rhodes looked at her as if he suddenly realized he wasn't the only person in the room.

"No questions. I'll start working on this right now and let you know what I find," Tonya said.

"Great." He nodded in appreciation. "Thank you," he said as he was almost in his office.

"You're welcome." She smiled. He could be nice if he wanted to be.

She was still researching and taking notes when six o'clock rolled around. He came out of his office and stood there silently. When she finally looked up, she saw him watching her.

"Can I help you with something?" she asked politely.

"Thank you for your hard work," he said sincerely.

Tonya looked at him uncertainly. He was hard to read. He was nice to her on the phone, but whenever he got within eyesight, his demeanor changed into a grouch.

The funny thing was, he didn't seem to have this problem with clients. He was friendly with everyone who came to see him. Except her.

Maybe she imagined it. He was being nice enough right now.

She shrugged her shoulders and said, "No problem."

They left the office together an hour later. Tonya took a detour and stopped for coffee. When she arrived at the Sheffield's house, the lawyer's car was already there. He was standing next to it, holding his briefcase, and waiting for her. He waved when he saw her and gestured for her to park behind him.

As she walked up to him, she was reminded again of how attractive he was. Maybe it was the sunlight, which made him look friendlier and more approachable. His blue eyes seemed to sparkle outside. It was a good thing there were two feet between them. Otherwise, he'd be irresistible even though she was working for him and had only known him for a week.

"Thank you for coming out here," he said with a genuine smile.

She could feel herself blush under his gaze. Was he checking her out, or was she imagining things? She looked at her shoes momentarily.

He asked, "Are you ready?"

When she looked up again, he was still watching her. She suddenly felt tongue-tied and merely nodded and followed him to the front door.

The Sheffields received them warmly and repeatedly offered tea and coffee, which they declined. The elderly couple invited them to take a seat on the small couch next to each other. It was awkward, but Tonya couldn't exactly tell them about the two-foot-rule to avoid being seated next to her employer. His knee touched hers more than once, even though he was visibly trying to keep his distance.

It felt like she was doing something forbidden, sitting next to him like this. Like the time she smoked behind the house as a teenager and hoped her parents wouldn't catch her. And yet, she wasn't doing anything wrong this time. It was just his silly rule, which made her feel like this.

"We can't get up from the couch easily. You must forgive us for choosing these chairs instead," Mrs. Sheffield said as she lowered herself into the chair facing them.

"Thank you for inviting us. You have such a beautiful home," Patrick said.

He wasn't exaggerating. The exterior of the house looked much like every other house in the neighborhood, resembling the cottage style popular in the seventies. Inside, it was a different story. There were knickknacks and heirlooms everywhere. In the midst of it, she spied several bronze sculptures resembling Greek gods and goddesses, including Zeus, Athena, and Poseidon.

"Where did you get those sculptures?" Tonya asked.

"We brought them with us from our Europe tour. Greece was my favorite country to visit." Mrs. Sheffield smiled, pleased someone appreciated her collection.

"I've always wanted to go to Greece," Tonya said, suddenly excited. "Where did you go?"

"We've been to Athens, of course," Mrs. Sheffield said. "It was part of a big city tour."

"We also spent some time on Crete," Mr. Sheffield said.

Tonya's eyes lit up. "Did you see the caverns Zeus was born in?"

"Yes, we did." Mrs. Sheffield smiled. "I think we have some pictures I can show you."

"Maybe another time," Patrick's deep voice interrupted.

Tonya almost glared at him.

"You're quite right," said Mrs. Sheffield. "Reminiscing is fun, but of course we have other things to discuss, and we don't want to waste your time."

"We sure have accumulated a lot of things over the years," Mr. Sheffield said, looking around as if he was discovering his treasures just now.

"Well, we have lived here for forty years, now. Isn't that right, Harold?" Mrs. Sheffield addressed her husband sweetly.

Mr. Sheffield nodded.

"Was this house newly built when you moved in?" Tonya couldn't help but ask more questions, even though she could sense Mr. Rhodes getting fidgety next to her.

"Yes. We were one of the first people to move into this neighborhood. We planted all the trees, and we even helped some of our neighbors move in." Mr. Sheffield coughed. "A few of them still live here, too."

"That's neat," Mr. Rhodes said.

He was listening attentively, which was an excellent quality in a lawyer. But Tonya was sure he hadn't come here for a history lesson on this neighborhood, and Mrs. Sheffield seemed to pick up on it, too.

"I'm sure you're not interested in all this, Mr. Rhodes. What do you need to know to help us with our problem?" Mrs. Sheffield turned her intelligent, blue eyes on him.

"Can you tell us more about the young man who came here that day?" Mr. Rhodes asked.

Mr. and Mrs. Sheffield did their best to describe the man they had seen. Tonya took notes diligently, but she had little hopes their description would lead them anywhere. The young man was probably long gone. Presumably, he didn't even live in Texas. He had given them his business card, which didn't include a picture. Tonya examined it carefully and asked to keep it to make a copy.

"We don't need it, dear. Please just take it." Mrs. Sheffield waved her hands. "I would like to forget about it all."

Mr. Sheffield reached out, touched his wife's hand, and patted it gently.

Tonya noticed the sweet gesture. These two didn't have a mansion or a fancy car or any savings to speak of, and yet, they still had something Tonya envied. They loved each other after all these years. A blind person could have seen and felt the genuine affection they had for each other. Would she ever have this kind of bond with someone?

"Could you give us a list of your neighbors who may have fallen for this scam, too? We'd like to help them if possible," Patrick Rhodes said.

He had used just the right tone, helpful and compassionate at the same time. He was sincere in his desire to right this wrong, Tonya was sure of it.

"I already made a list for you." Mrs. Sheffield handed a piece of paper to Tonya.

"Is this your handwriting? It's beautiful," Tonya admired the paper. It held a list of a dozen names in elaborate cursive writing.

"Will you be able to read it? I forget people don't learn cursive anymore these days."

"I can read it just fine." She would not tell Mrs. Sheffield people were barely writing by hand at all.

"What will happen now?" Mr. Sheffield asked.

"I'm glad you asked. Miss Corley has already done some preliminary research." Patrick smiled kindly. "This seems to be a known scam. We're going to work hard and get in touch with the responsible party. In the meantime, we'll ask you to sign a contract with us to retain our services."

Mr. Rhodes pulled out some paperwork from his briefcase. When Tonya saw the Sheffields exchange confused looks with each other, she almost rolled her eyes at her boss. These two needed more details.

"Until we know who's behind it, we can't tell you if we can recover your money for you. But we will try everything we can. Before we can take action on your behalf, you have to hire us to work for you and represent you. That's what the contract is for," Tonya said.

She took the paperwork from the lawyer and got up to kneel between the Sheffields. She read every paragraph of the two-page contract out loud to them and explained all the finer points. She didn't want them to feel overwhelmed or confused.

"As far as fees go, we're taking this case on a contingency basis. It means you don't have to pay us anything to work for you. We only get paid if we can recover any money for you. Mr. Rhodes will receive thirty-five percent if the case goes to court. If we settle before a trial, it would reduce his percentage to twenty-five percent," Tonya explained. "If we don't succeed, then we don't get paid at all. It means we have the same goal: to help you recuperate your losses."

Mr. Sheffield nodded.

"I will leave this contract here with you. I want you to read it again carefully, think it over, maybe take it to someone you trust. You're welcome to get another opinion, too. We want you to feel comfortable with this decision."

Mrs. Sheffield said, "Thank you, dear, but we have discussed this in great lengths already. We're ready to sign."

Tonya looked at Mr. Sheffield, and he nodded.

Ten minutes later, Tonya and Patrick Rhodes stood on the sidewalk, the signed contract in her hand.

"Great job, Miss Corley," he said, admiration in his voice.

"Thanks." She looked at the paperwork. "You know what struck me most about this couple?"

He looked at her, intrigued.

"Neither of them tried to blame the other for what happened. They each blamed themselves for trusting this guy, but there was no finger-pointing."

"Maybe that's their secret sauce to marital happiness."

"Maybe."

"Are you ready to do this again with the neighbors?"

She exhaled. "Yes, let's do it."

On the way to the first house, Tonya asked, "Is this going to become a class-action lawsuit?"

"I hope not. The only people who stand to benefit in those are the lawyers."

She chuckled. "Did you forget you're a lawyer?"

"Of course not," he said. "Don't get me wrong. I'd love the money. But I'll get paid for these cases one at a time, too. But our clients will only get what they deserve if we don't lump them all together in one big lawsuit."

This was a side of him she hadn't seen yet. Suddenly, he almost came across as more of a philanthropist than a lawyer. Tonya followed him to the next house while she thought about what he had said. He was trying to balance earning more money and meeting the clients' needs. The lawyers she had worked for in the past had no such misgivings. They would always choose the money unless the client was a family member or a friend.

But if Patrick was such a nice guy, why was he rude to her? Before she could think it through, the door opened and an elderly gentleman greeted them.

Patrick and Tonya spent the rest of the evening talking to various neighbors. By nine o'clock, Tonya's stomach was rumbling, and her list had eleven names and addresses. As they walked back to where they had parked, she felt an immense sense of satisfaction. Tonya finally had the feeling she was doing something real, something that mattered.

"I can't believe how much money these people have lost," Mr. Rhodes said.

Tonya nodded in agreement. It was nice to see how much he cared about his clients. She hadn't even realized he was thinking about any of them on a personal level. But still. He was a lawyer, and every case meant income for him.

He continued, "Take the Sheffields, for example. They lost all their retirement savings. There's nothing left, even though they've worked for decades and saved up a lot."

"You're right."

"Of course I'm right. I'm a lawyer." He smirked. "But you know something? The Sheffields didn't let it get them down. They're still happy."

"They seem happy. They have each other."

"Too bad love can't feed you."

She would not stand around and talk to her employer about love. Time to change the subject.

"Speaking of feeding people," Tonya said as she looked at her watch. "I'm hungry, and I think we've knocked on enough doors for the day."

"Yes, we have."

"I'll see you on Monday?"

"Yes, see you Monday," he said.

She walked to her car and unlocked the door.

"And thanks again for coming out today," he called out to her right.

She waved and got behind the steering wheel. She couldn't quite decide what she thought about him. One minute, she could see his brain calculating twenty-five percent of a half-a-million dollars, and the next moment he was deeply upset about the people who lost everything to a scam artist.

He was still a lawyer. He would get some nice commissions for these cases. And if Tonya played her cards right, she would benefit right alongside him.

Chapter 3

"I DON'T REALLY UNDERSTAND why you want to become a lawyer when you already work for one, Tonya," Darlene Corley said as she inspected a tomato for bruises.

The supermarket was crowded today, and Tonya's goal was to leave the store while her mother seemed to want to touch every item they sold. Tonya sighed inwardly as she put a bunch of bananas into their cart.

"I already told you why I want to do this. I want to help people."

"Law school is expensive."

"I'm applying for scholarships, Mom, to reduce the cost of school."

"What about rent and food? I don't think you want to move back home," Darlene said as she pushed her cart along. "Now if you had a husband, it would be easier. He could support you."

"I don't plan to move back home," Tonya said.

As much as she wanted to go to law school, moving back home would be too big of a price to pay. If she stayed with her parents, she would have to endure her mother's snide remarks about marriage and children every day. As it was, Tonya found it difficult enough to ignore them once a week.

"Oh dear, these bananas are too ripe. They'll just go bad in a day."

Darlene clucked her tongue and turned the cart around. She replaced the fruit and picked out a bunch of bananas identical to the ones Tonya had grabbed a moment ago. Tonya took a deep breath in and out. Every grocery trip was this way with her mother. Tonya really didn't understand why she got dragged into going time and again.

"What else is on your list?" Tonya peered over her mother's shoulder to decipher her scribbled notes.

"I need batteries, toilet paper, and bread," Darlene said without looking at her list. "Look at these cute muffins."

"Yours are much better, Mom," Tonya said.

She wasn't lying, but couldn't her mother just shop like normal people? Instead, she acted like a kid in the candy store each time, looking at every aisle and displaying unusual excitement for baked goods she never purchased.

"I saw your aunt the other day," Darlene said while slowly navigating the cart through the cake displays.

"Really? How is she?"

"I don't know. We didn't talk. I saw her at the store, but she vanished before I could get closer."

"Do you think she saw you?"

"Of course. She wants nothing to do with me or anyone else from our family." Darlene sounded hurt.

"When was the last time you talked to her?"

"I catch a glimpse of her now and then—it's a small town, you know. But it's been many years since we've talked."

"I don't think it's us, Mom. She fears…"

"Well, you may be right. But there's nothing we can do."

"If Aunt Allyson had legal representation, we could prevent him from ever going near her. She could get a divorce, change her name, and start a new life," Tonya said with conviction.

"Aunt Allyson doesn't want help, Tonya. Otherwise, she would have turned to her family. You don't think we would have gladly paid for her lawyer?" Darlene suddenly looked angry.

"Of course." Tonya felt chastised. She had never blamed her mother for Aunt Allyson's circumstances, had she?

"Well, you don't know the whole story."

"What don't I know, Mom?"

Suddenly, Darlene's face was smiling again. "Oh look, batteries are on sale. That's just wonderful, isn't it?"

***

Tonya anxiously peered at the time on the dashboard as she accelerated on the highway. She might just get to work on time if she didn't get stuck behind a tractor. Fortunately, the street seemed clear of slow-moving vehicles this morning.

She exhaled deeply when she heard a sudden loud bang. Unless someone was shooting at her, there was something seriously wrong with her vehicle.

She found her warning light button and carefully steered her car onto the side of the road. When the car had come to a stop, she turned off the engine and suppressed the stream of curse words bubbling up inside her.

Tonya climbed through the car and got out on the passenger side. Cars whizzed by as she surveyed the damage.

The tire on the rear was flat as a pancake. Great. Just what she needed when she was already cutting it close to get to work on time.

Her phone rang. *Patrick Rhodes.* Of all people. She answered briskly.

"Where is the paperwork for the neighbors?"

"I haven't filed it. Should be sitting on my desk." Someone honked at another car for getting cut off. Tonya covered her other ear to focus on the conversation with the lawyer. "I might be a little late."

"Are you on the road? What happened?"

"Just a little car trouble." It spelled big trouble to replace the tire, but he didn't need to know that.

"Where exactly are you?"

"I'm on 46, on the side of the road. I should be at the office within an hour." She suppressed a sigh of frustration. "I'm sorry. I'll make up the time this evening."

"Let me help you. I can be there in ten minutes," he said.

"No, it's fine. I've got it all under control."

"Really?"

"Yes, really."

She shook her head in annoyance after she hung up. He didn't think she could change a tire. How difficult could it be?

She opened the browser on her phone. How to change a tire. Lug nuts. Jack up car. Switch tire. Easy peasy. She could do this.

She dropped the phone on the front seat and opened the trunk. It didn't take long to find the tools and the spare tire, although her blouse was no longer white after she had set everything on the ground. At least, the problematic tire was facing away from the busy road.

This was one of those times when it would have been nice to have a boyfriend, although she had never had a handy boyfriend. Nick, the cheater, had liked cars well enough, but he wouldn't have come to her rescue. He'd probably have called it emancipating her.

She had the car jacked up in no time. That wasn't so hard. She almost congratulated herself. But then it came to loosening the lug nuts. She tried all of them, but they wouldn't budge. She was sweating now and cursing inwardly.

A car pulled up behind her. Relief flooded through her. Finally, someone was nice enough to rescue her.

To her surprise, it was Patrick.

"What are you doing here?" She felt immediately defensive.

"I came to help," he said.

"I don't need help. I got everything I need." She rose, careful to avoid touching her clothes with her smeared hands any more than necessary.

He took in the situation at a glance. "Can't get the lug nuts off, can you?"

She grimaced. "I just got started."

He crouched down and lowered the jack again.

"What are you doing?" She bent to touch his arm, determined not to let him undo the hard work she had already done.

He froze and turned his head to look at her. Slowly, she removed her hand from his arm. She hadn't been this close to him before, thanks to his stupid two-foot rule. Her cheeks felt hot under his gaze.

She stammered, "It took some effort to get the tire jacked up." Why did she suddenly feel so incompetent around him?

He cleared his throat. "Lug nuts can be a pain to get off. You'll need leverage to loosen them. If the tire's spinning, it makes it harder."

She bit her lip. That sounded very logical. Why hadn't she thought of it herself? Maybe Google had mentioned lug nuts first, and she hadn't followed directions.

"Do you want to try it now?" he asked her.

She shook her head. "I believe you."

With apparent ease, he loosened the lug nuts and jacked up the car again.

"My dad taught me and my sister how to change a tire before we could even drive," Patrick said, nostalgia in his voice. "He tried hard to be there for us after Mom died. I think he read a book on what you should know before you move out, and he ticked off every item on the list." He chuckled.

She was pleasantly surprised at seeing this side of him. Patrick seemed like a nice guy. Maybe he hid his feelings beneath his grouchy exterior. It couldn't have been easy to lose his mother.

"My father always had roadside assistance. He probably knows how to change a tire, but he never taught me." Tonya tried to remember car troubles from when she was younger, but nothing came to mind. Her parents always drove newer cars.

Ten minutes later, Patrick was done. He got to his feet and put the tire in the trunk.

His hand touched hers when she took the jack from him and placed it in the trunk. She stepped back as if he had burned her.

"Thank you. I appreciate your help," she said.

"No problem." He frowned as he examined her old tire. "You need to get new tires. This one is completely bald."

"I will. Soon," she said.

"It's not safe to drive like that," he admonished her. "You're lucky you didn't get hurt."

She closed the trunk and made to move past him, but he touched her arm, making her look up at him.

"Seriously, this is important." He sounded angry now. "You could have died with a blowout on the freeway."

She was touched by his concern for her. "Thanks again."

"I'll see you at the office."

***

Tonya got to work early the next day. She had to drive slowly with her spare tire, which is why she had left with plenty of time to spare. All four tires needed to be replaced as soon as possible, but she had been grappling with how to pay for it. She didn't want to ask her parents, but she didn't want to max out her credit card, either. For now, she'd concentrate on work.

With a key to the office, she didn't have to wait for Mr. Rhodes to let her in. She unlocked the front door and propped it open, leaving the exterior glass door in place. For a place of business, a glass door made sense. It allowed people to enter without feeling like the house was closed, but it prevented the owner from air conditioning the outside.

As soon as her computer started up, she dug into her research. She was so engrossed she didn't hear her employer come down the stairs until he spoke to her. "How long have you been here?"

Tonya looked up. He seemed just as surprised to see her there as she was to see him.

"Just a little over an hour. I found something on Cobblestone Investments."

"Good," he said as he sat on the couch across from her. "Let's hear it."

"Have you ever heard of Parachute Executives?"

Patrick shook his head. "It sounds familiar, but I can't place them. Tell me more."

"Parachute Executives recently acquired Cobblestone Investments. It looks like they didn't do their research before the merger. There's already a list of complaints about Cobblestone on the Internet. Since Parachute owns them, they're liable for all of it."

"How big is Parachute Executives?"

"They're huge. They have over three thousand employees in offices all over the country. Their reported net revenue was fifteen billion dollars last year. They make money by buying and selling other companies. Only this time, they bought the wrong firm." Tonya took a moment to let it sink in. "Their corporate offices are in Savannah, Georgia."

Patrick's eyes lit up. "I think I know where."

Tonya looked at him, confused. Hadn't he just said he couldn't even place them?

"I've seen the building. It's huge and kind of ruins the skyline." Patrick shrugged and explained further, "I've been to Savannah plenty of times. I have relatives there."

Tonya nodded and glanced at him. He didn't have the Southern drawl she associated with Georgia. He didn't sound like a Texan, either.

Patrick suddenly seemed eager to make a move. "Let's send them our demand letter."

Tonya retorted, "We haven't finalized the demand letter yet."

"Get it done and send it with an overnight courier today."

"Okay."

She opened up her word processor and started typing. A minute later, she looked over at the couch. Why was Patrick still sitting there watching her?

Before she could ask, her cell phone rang. She cursed herself for not silencing it earlier.

"Answer it if you must," he said as he finally got up and walked away to his office.

She picked up the phone.

"Hi Tonya, I wanted to ask you what kind of paperwork you need from me. I'm getting an escort to my house today to grab some of my things."

It was Sabrina's quiet voice on the other line, and Tonya instantly felt a stab of guilt. She had done nothing for Sabrina. She hadn't even arranged for legal representation for her yet.

Tonya lowered her voice. "If you can get birth certificates and social security numbers for you and your son, it will really help. Financial information is also useful. Bank statements or paychecks, stuff like that."

"Are you at work? I don't want to interrupt," Sabrina said.

"It's fine. This is more important. Are you leaving right now?"

"No, but we're going before noon to make sure we can get in and out without causing trouble," Sabrina said.

Sabrina's voice sounded matter-of-fact, but Tonya could only imagine how scared she must feel. Presumably, her husband was at work, which is why they had chosen that time. But he could come home for lunch, leave work early, or call in sick. Tonya reeled in her thoughts. Being nervous on Sabrina's behalf didn't help anyone.

"The more information we have, the better. But if it's a document he'll miss, such as an old tax return, you can make copies and someone will return it for you. If I think of anything else, I'll call you."

The call ended and Tonya turned her attention back to her screen.

"Boyfriend?"

Tonya turned around. Patrick Rhodes had walked back into the room and was now standing about three feet behind her desk. How much of her conversation had he overheard?

She shook her head slowly. Now was the time to talk about Sabrina and get him to take the case.

"No, it was a friend of mine, Sabrina. She's staying at the women's shelter, and she really needs a lawyer."

Tonya watched Patrick for a reaction, but he hadn't even been listening.

"Can we talk about Sabrina's case? She needs a lawyer who works pro bono," Tonya said.

"Pro bono?" Now she had his attention. Patrick looked at her incredulously. "Pro bono cases don't pay the bills."

What happened to caring about his clients?

"I know," Tonya said. "Look, this will be easy. I'll do all the work. You just have to sign the papers."

"What kind of case is this?"

"She has an abusive husband. She's hiding at the shelter with her child. A restraining order has been filed, but she needs a divorce, sole custody, and child support."

Patrick seemed to give the matter some thought. She was about to make a persuasive argument when he spoke.

"Fine. But you're handling the details."

"Thank you," Tonya said as Patrick Rhodes closed his office door behind him.

When Tonya left for home in the evening, her car wasn't in the spot she had parked it. In a panic, she looked around. Had someone stolen her vehicle?

This was just awful. Why had she complained about buying new tires? Now she didn't even have a car.

In a daze, she walked back inside. What would she do now? Call the cops?

"Hey, did you forget something?" Patrick strode out of his office as she shut the front door behind her.

"My car's gone." She could feel tears forming. This was one hell of a week.

"Oh, right. I forgot. Follow me."

Bewildered, she followed him out the door to the garage. As the door opened automatically, she shot him a confused look.

"What's my car doing in your garage?"

"I had them put on new tires." He frowned. "You came to work with that donut again today. I took care of it."

"This is incredible." She didn't know what to say to this. His gruff demeanor reminded her to keep her distance, but she felt like hugging him. New tires! He was such a nice guy, and she was absolutely wrong about him.

"They did an alignment, too. Just so you know. You should be good to go." He pulled her keys out of his pocket and threw them to her. "You might need these."

"You stole my keys?"

"In my defense, you left them on your desk." He smirked. "Drive safely."

"I'll pay you back," she said.

He waved her off. "No need. Can't have you show up late to work every time a tire blows out. It's cheaper to do this than have you miss client phone calls."

Maybe he wasn't a nice guy, and her initial impression hadn't been wrong. He valued money over everything else.

Before she could respond, he walked back to the front door. She took the hint, got in the car, and reversed out of the garage.

Chapter 4

AS TONYA TURNED into the parking lot of her apartment complex, her phone rang. She checked the display. Victoria.

They had texted a few times since Victoria's last call, but Tonya still hadn't seen her friend since the morning of her canceled wedding. Tonya pushed the answer button.

They talked about nonconsequential things for a few minutes, and then Victoria got to the point.

"I was wondering... would you like to come to dinner tonight? I'm making lasagna and Piña coladas."

"I don't know, Vicky," Tonya hedged.

"Come on, Tonya. Please. Just give me a chance to make it up to you," Victoria pleaded.

Tonya had to smile despite herself. Victoria knew her better than anyone. This was a peace offering by her best friend, which Tonya couldn't reject. Drinking Piña coladas had been their thing before the debacle with Mark happened. If she was going to forgive and forget, Tonya would prefer to do it over her favorite beverage.

Of course, she would go. How could she not? This was her best friend. "Alright, I'll be there."

If she hurried, she still had time to work on her scholarship applications before heading over to Victoria's place.

An hour later, Tonya sighed as she reluctantly closed her laptop. Her list included several scholarships to apply for, but she still hadn't found the time to submit the paperwork. She really should stay home and make some progress on this front.

It would be easy to cancel on Victoria. She had a legitimate reason. But if she was honest with herself, she missed her friend. She missed having someone to confide in. A lot had happened since Mark had stood her up at the altar.

An hour later, Tonya parked her car in Victoria's driveway. She would have recognized Victoria's little Chevy anywhere.

Victoria opened the door and grinned. "I'm glad you came, Tonya."

"Me, too," Tonya said as she closed the gap between them and hugged Victoria.

"Are you okay?" Victoria looked at her friend closely.

Tonya smiled. "You know what? I think I am."

Victoria sighed in relief.

"But I'm starving," Tonya added.

"Come on in. Dinner is almost done."

Once in the kitchen, Victoria handed her a Piña colada, and Tonya promptly took a big sip. Victoria busied herself at the stove, and the smell of lasagna made Tonya's stomach growl.

"How are things going with Mr. Mark Perfect? Are you getting a dog yet?" Tonya asked, not able to keep jealousy out of her voice.

Tonya clasped her hand over her mouth, shocked at her own resentment. Maybe she still held a grudge against Victoria without realizing it.

Victoria sighed. "I didn't mean to hurt you. But you weren't in love with him. You said so yourself."

The *Perfect* Plan

"That's not the point, Vicky. You're supposed to be my friend and not steal my future husband."

Tonya realized her voice sounded whiny, but she couldn't help herself. It suddenly struck her as unfair Vicky had someone where she was alone again.

"If it helps, it's going great. Mark is amazing," Victoria smirked, clearly trying to lighten the mood.

Tonya rolled her eyes, and they sat in silence for a while. Alcohol always loosened Tonya's tongue and before long, more truths spilled out.

"I could have used a friend, you know."

"I know, Tonya. I tried to talk to you, but you ignored my calls."

"What would you have done in my shoes?" Tonya asked.

Victoria pondered the question in silence. Then she grinned and said, "I don't know, but not marrying for money could be a start."

Tonya laughed out loud. "That's hilarious coming from you."

And suddenly, her heart felt lighter. Victoria had spent the last several years matching the daughters of rich parents with suitable—meaning rich—husbands. Love had never entered into the equation. And then Victoria had fallen in love with Mark—the guy she had matched with Tonya. Cruel irony.

"Are you still looking for a husband, Tonya?"

"No." Tonya shook her head. "I'm applying for scholarships."

"Good for you," Victoria said. "How are things going?"

Tonya sighed, feeling content for the first time since she had stepped through the front door. It felt good to have someone to confide in.

"Let's see. You already know I got a new job. My employer is a lawyer named Patrick Rhodes, who is insanely hot."

Victoria giggled.

"My mom keeps telling me I need to get married. Nothing new there… She tried to hook me up with Daron."

Victoria whistled. "Daron is cute. And why not him? We both know he has a crush on you."

Tonya shrugged. "I'm just not interested. He reminds me of a puppy. We've been texting. He's hard to shake."

"Daron's a good guy," Victoria said. "The lawyer, then? Since he's so hot."

Tonya shrugged noncommittally. By now, she could admit to herself she had a crush on her boss. But it was innocent, like having a crush on a teacher. It wasn't a viable option for a genuine relationship.

Victoria got up to serve dinner and refill their Piña coladas. Tonya sniffed her food in appreciation and almost burned her tongue on the first bite.

Victoria pulled her out of her reverie. "Tell me more about the lawyer you work for. Is he a nice guy?"

Tonya grimaced. "He's a real grouch, but around his clients he's nice enough."

He was more than nice to his clients. He could have made a killing with a class-action lawsuit, but he had pursued each case individually instead.

Why was she suddenly defending her opinion of Patrick Rhodes? Maybe the alcohol made her feel kindly disposed toward him.

"If he's such a grouch, why do you have that look on your face?"

"What look?"

"You know," Victoria said.

Tonya blushed. "He's hot, Vicky. I wouldn't kick him out of bed if he wasn't my employer."

Maybe she should have stopped after the second Piña colada.

"Really?" Victoria grinned as she pulled out her phone. "I want to see this hot employer of yours."

The *Perfect* Plan

Tonya leaned back in her chair. "Nothing good comes from looking people up. Remember that's how everything started with Mark."

"Not from my point of view," Victoria said with a smirk. "I probably would have never met him otherwise. Check this out!" Her tone changed from joking to downright shocked.

"What? What is it?"

Tonya leaned over her best friend's shoulder to see what the search engine had revealed about Patrick. There was a class picture of him during law school. She remembered seeing it when she looked him up before the interview. But Victoria's finger pointed at the link to a YouTube video titled "Most Embarrassing Breakups of All Times".

"Why would his name show up there?" Tonya asked.

Victoria shrugged. "Only one way to find out."

A feeling of dread came over Tonya. Based on the title, this was something Patrick would want to keep quiet. And even though Tonya was pretty sure he didn't want her to see this, she was equally sure she *had* to see the video. Victoria had already hit play and didn't give her a choice in the matter.

The video comprised lots of brief clips. The first showed a woman holding hands with a guy in a mall when another man approached them, clearly angry she was seeing someone else. Then the woman nonchalantly broke up with the jilted boyfriend and continued her shopping spree, leaving the other man staring at her, much to the amusement of the person behind the camera.

The next video showed a woman finishing a half marathon, beaming with pride. But as she walked away to cool down, her partner approached her with the dubious words of 'We need to talk.' A moment later, they could hear the woman screaming obscenities off camera.

Victoria chuckled. "This is hilarious. Let me get some popcorn."

Victoria paused the video and rummaged in her cabinet for popcorn. By the time the microwave dinged, she had opened the incriminating video on her laptop on the coffee table in the living room. It felt almost like any other movie night they had spent at Victoria's house.

"You know, the longer it takes to see your lawyer, the more of a spectacle his breakup will be. They always save the best for last to make you watch the entire video." Victoria carried a bowl of popcorn and put it between herself and Tonya on the couch with a flourish.

"He's not *my* lawyer. I just work for him," Tonya corrected her.

Victoria waved away her objections.

They watched the beginning of the video again. Tonya had to admit her friend was right. The breakups really got worse in almost every clip. She cringed as she watched a guy break up with his girlfriend over Thanksgiving dinner with the extended family. What could be worse than that?

"Wow, it must be one hell of a breakup," Victoria said, echoing Tonya's thoughts.

And suddenly, there was Patrick, as handsome as ever in slacks and a button-up shirt. Tonya sucked in her breath. He was sitting in a crowded stadium, watching a game.

"That's him," she whispered.

Victoria whistled. "He really is hot."

Tonya's eyes didn't leave the screen, although she wanted to avert her gaze. Whatever was about to happen would not be good. The camera zoomed out a little, showing a hot blond chick in a tank top and miniskirt next to him. They made quite the couple.

"She kinda looks like you," Victoria said.

As the camera zoomed in, Tonya could see a bit of a resemblance. The woman was blond, although her blond had definitely come from a bottle. The camera moved to the giant scoreboard on the field as the announcer's voice urged the audience to pay attention. They could see

Patrick and the blond chick on the scoreboard. He was now on his knees in front of her.

"She's going to say *no* to a public proposal?" Victoria squealed.

"If she had said yes, they probably wouldn't include it here," Tonya said dryly.

The rest of the clip played in slow motion as the blond rejected the proposal and all color drained from Patrick's face. The camera reverted to the scoreboard, where a 'congratulations to the happy couple' sign flickered for a second before someone switched it to the halftime score.

"Wow." It explained Patrick's behavior. "He didn't want to hire me at first. I thought it had something to do with the way I looked or that I was a woman."

"I'm not surprised," Victoria said, rewinding the clip and pausing on the image of the woman. "Look at this video. If I was him, I'd never speak to another woman again, much less hire one."

It was no wonder Patrick probably hated her guts.

"Oh well," Victoria laughed. "Even if it wasn't for her publicly dumping him, I would suggest you forget about him if you want to keep your job."

Tonya nodded in agreement. Vicky had nailed it. Getting involved with Patrick would only get her in trouble.

***

Tonya showed up to work early every day. She always had a lot of research and writing tasks, and it was impossible to do it all while clients showed up. Fortunately, she didn't mind putting in the hours, because the work was fun.

Most mornings, Tonya stopped by at the coffee shop to get a cup of latte macchiato because she couldn't stand the regular coffee at the office. Still, the coffee never went to waste. She brewed several pots every day for the clients who came to see Patrick.

She really shouldn't think of him as Patrick. It was Mr. Rhodes to her. But as long as she didn't slip up in conversation with him, she would be fine.

Patrick seemed to be in a chipper mood when he came downstairs.

"What are you working on this morning?" he asked as he loitered around her desk.

"Research. I have some dirt on the Sheffield case," Tonya said.

The phone rang before he could respond. Tonya automatically picked it up on the first ring.

"This is Marlene from Parachute Executives. I would like to arrange a phone conference between Jack Hayes and Patrick Rhodes."

Parachute Executives. This was it. Tonya grinned but kept her voice calm.

"Hello Marlene. Is Jack Hayes the lead lawyer on the case?" Tonya knew Patrick wouldn't want to speak to anyone else.

"Yes, ma'am. I have an appointment this afternoon at two Eastern time."

Tonya looked at the calendar. If Parachute Executives wanted a meeting right away, surely that was a good sign? Patrick Rhodes was supposed to go over Sabrina's paperwork, but Tonya would just take care of it and have him look through it later.

"Two o'clock should work. Let me give you his direct line to call," Tonya said.

The rest of the day went by in a flurry, as always. Clients came and went, and Tonya prepared several documents for various cases.

It was four in the afternoon when Patrick came out of his office. He looked thoughtful, and Tonya immediately wondered about his conversation with Jack Hayes.

"How was your meeting?"

"It was good. Parachute Executives has some very talented staff. But our case is strong," he said.

"What's the next step?"

"They want to meet. In person," he said.

"Where will the meeting take place? In Neuenhagen?"

It was a good guess on her part. Few attorneys made the trip to small-town Radfield when Neuenhagen had more to offer in terms of restaurants and other meeting venues.

"No. We'll meet at their headquarters in Savannah, Georgia."

"Okay," Tonya said as she pulled up his calendar. "When will you leave?"

"They're flying us out, putting us up in a nice hotel room overnight. This is the case I've been waiting for. I can feel it." Patrick grinned as he rubbed his hands together.

"Us?" Tonya frowned at him.

"Yes," he said. "I need you to come with me."

"That's a lot of overtime," she said.

"You'll get paid for a regular workday. Sleeping in a hotel room isn't working. And all expenses are paid." Before she could object, he continued. "Come on. You're getting a cut of the settlement. Isn't it in your best interest to move this case along?"

He was right. And it could be fun. She had never traveled for work before. This is what it would be like to be a real lawyer, too.

She could get excited about it. "I'm in. When are we leaving?"

"We're flying out next Tuesday morning and coming back Wednesday night."

She nodded slowly.

She would go to Savannah. This could be a lot of fun. She wasn't going to Greece by any means, but Savannah was a beautiful Southern city. It would be worth a visit. Maybe she'd have time to explore in the evening. She could always sleep on the plane.

"What are you thinking about?"

Tonya came out of her daydream for a moment and noticed Patrick staring at her. She could feel her cheeks get hot.

"Nothing. Just the trip. I've never been to Savannah. I hear it's beautiful."

"It is." He smiled genuinely, amused by her enthusiasm. "I think you'd love it there."

She raised her eyebrows questioningly. How would he know what she liked and didn't like? He seemed to guess what she was thinking.

"If you want to visit places like Athens and Crete, you appreciate older cities." He shrugged. "Savannah is about as old as you get in the United States. Many of the people who settled in Savannah in the late eighteenth century also imitated Greek architecture."

She stared at him, astonished. Her own mother didn't listen closely enough to know how much she cared about anything to do with Greece. But before she could say anything, Patrick had walked back to his office and shut the door behind him.

Chapter 5

WHEN TONYA SHOWED UP at work the next day, she was yawning. She had spent too much time looking at pictures of Savannah online. She knew it was silly to get worked up over a two-day trip, which would probably involve a lot of boring meetings, but she just couldn't help it. And a little lack of sleep would not destroy her good mood this morning.

Just as she had settled in and responded to her first email, Patrick came out of the office again. *Mr. Rhodes*, she reminded herself. She could not accidentally use his first name, or all hell would break loose.

"Do you have any plans this evening?" he asked in his usual brisk manner.

Tonya hesitated.

"I take that as a no. Will you come to dinner with me and a colleague of mine to discuss the Sheffield case?"

Tonya hesitated. "I could have plans."

"Of course, you could have any number of plans. But you hesitated." He treated her to that charming smile of his, which he normally reserved for his clients.

"What if I don't want to go to dinner with you?" God forbid she stared at him throughout dinner. Why was she attracted to her employer, of all people?

Besides, this was not what she had bargained for when she signed up for this job. It was enough she used her weekends to help with the Sheffield case.

"I realize it's a lot to ask."

"It's way too much to ask," Tonya said.

His ocean-blue eyes pleaded with her. "You can pick the restaurant and order whatever you like."

"I'll have lobster *and* steak," she said.

"It's a deal. I'll even order champagne for you to wash your hands in." His eyes had a twinkle in them as he grinned at her, suddenly sure of his victory. "You'll come, won't you?"

She laughed. He could be very persuasive when he wanted something. And there was no harm in going to dinner with him and a colleague. It sounded more exciting than applying for scholarships, and she wouldn't have to pay.

"You owe me. You owe me big time."

"Dinner's on me," he said graciously.

"That goes without saying," Tonya said. "But what's in it for me?"

"I'll buy you a drink."

"Then I'd be drinking and driving," she said.

"I'll pick you up."

Was this a good idea? Getting in the car with her boss, who refused to even shake hands with her? Then again, it was just a business dinner. Why not?

"Wait, where will I sit? I'm not sitting in the trunk to satisfy your two-foot rule." Tonya glared at him defiantly.

He laughed. "It's fine. We'll make an exception. It's not a long drive."

She didn't care. The two-foot rule was his invention, not hers.

***

The phone rang just as she put the finishing touches on her lipstick. Tonya put the call on speakerphone without interrupting her task. She had showered and changed into her little black dress for the occasion, determined to look more than presentable.

"Hi, Mom. What's up?"

"Nothing. Is it a crime to call my only child to see how she's doing? Do I always have to have a reason to call?"

"Of course not, Mom. It's just... I'm on my way out. Can I call you later?"

"Well, sure, but I wanted to tell you something I've heard."

Tonya sighed. If she wasn't careful, this could turn into a long-blown story about her mother meeting a long-lost cousin twice removed in the unlikeliest of places, and how said relative was now twice the size they used to be. Or had given birth to quadruplets.

The doorbell rang. This would be her employer now.

"What is it, Mom?" Tonya asked as she slipped into her shoes.

"It's about a scholarship. The name is Tyke Scholarship or something, and they offer a full ride to anyone they accept."

It wasn't much information to go on, but Tonya dutifully noted it down. The doorbell rang again, and Tonya hurried to open it. Patrick's stood, his mouth open, as if he was about to say something. But no sound came out, and he just stared at her.

"Thanks, Mom. I'll look into it," she said into the phone, hoping to end the conversation.

"No problem. I want to be supportive, Tonya."

"Thanks, I appreciate it. I'll call you later," Tonya resolutely ended the call, dropping the phone into her purse. Then she turned her attention to Patrick, who was still staring at her.

"What's wrong? Did you see a ghost?" Tonya looked down nervously. Did she have a big stain on her dress she hadn't noticed?

"Nothing is wrong," Patrick shook his head for a moment and cleared his throat. "I've just never seen you with your hair down."

There was an odd tone in his voice. They both looked at each other for a moment, and Tonya could feel the heat rising in her cheeks.

He looked rather sharp himself, but Tonya would not show him she was checking him out, too. It was no big deal, really. There was just something about a suit that turned desirable men into chick magnets. Patrick was no exception.

If he hadn't been her employer, she would have already made a move on him.

And it wasn't just about the suit. It was the way Patrick exuded confidence while still showing compassion for the less fortunate, like the Sheffields. And he cared enough to remember she liked Greek architecture. But nothing could happen between them, she reminded herself, as she tore her gaze away from him.

She broke the spell by jingling her keys. "Shall we?"

He nodded and led the way. As he walked down the stairs, she wondered what it would feel like to run her fingers through his hair.

What was wrong with her? She needed to get a grip on herself.

They drove to the restaurant in silence.

"Here we are," Patrick said as they pulled up to Marie's Steakhouse, a family-owned restaurant serving home-grown food. He looked at Tonya and said, "You're not a vegetarian, are you?"

"Nope. You promised me steak *and* lobster, remember?"

The smell of food made her stomach growl. This restaurant was an upscale place, too. Despite the hometown feel, it was way out of her price range. She couldn't wait to try the food.

The *Perfect* Plan

Patrick nodded slowly and smiled at her, and she momentarily forgot about food altogether. She wanted to ask him if he was on the menu, too, but fortunately, Patrick didn't give her a chance.

"Looks like good old Trevor beat us here," Patrick said.

It was immediately obvious who Trevor was. Only a lawyer or business executive would dress in an expensive suit and tie and talk on the phone instead of enjoying the balmy weather this evening. She could hear Trevor barking at someone on the phone, but he put it in his pocket when he saw them approaching. He smiled when he saw Tonya and shook her hand.

"Trevor, this is Tonya Corley. This is Trevor Simmons," Patrick introduced them.

"It's nice to meet you," Tonya said.

Trevor was half a head shorter than Patrick, but he looked like he spent all his spare time lifting weights or tanning. He reminded Tonya a little of her ex, Nick, the football player who had cheated on her.

Unlike Nick, Trevor was a gentleman and made small talk with Tonya while they waited to be seated. Patrick was unusually reserved and listened quietly. When Tonya glanced over, she caught him staring at her with an odd expression on his face.

Before she could include him in the conversation, the waitress appeared and led them to their table. After everyone ordered, things got serious.

"Let's hear it, Trevor. What's the big idea?" Patrick said.

"I heard about the Sheffield case you're working on. I recently signed up seven other cases just like it. I know there are more out there, because Radfield is full of retirees who want to bolster their nest eggs." Trevor smiled. "This is a goldmine for us. I think we should round them all up and hit Cobblestone with a class action suit."

Patrick nodded slowly. "You would think so."

"Just think about it. They'd pay out millions, and we'd rake a nice thirty-five percent off the top. We could escape the rat race. This is a lawyer's dream come true."

The waitress brought their drinks and Trevor downed half his beer immediately.

Patrick looked at Tonya. "What do you think about it?"

Tonya gnawed her lip. She didn't like where this was going, but it wasn't her decision. She wasn't the lawyer representing any of these people.

"How much would each client receive in this settlement scheme?" she asked, determined to reserve judgment.

Trevor shrugged. "Depends on how many millions Cobblestone will pay." He turned his attention to Patrick, "I think the Sheffields should be the lead plaintiffs since you're already in touch with Cobblestone."

It wasn't difficult to see Trevor was only interested in the profit side of the case.

"I brought Miss Corley here because she has met with the Sheffields and several other plaintiffs. I intend to recover the money they've lost, and I don't think it's as likely with a class action suit," Patrick said.

"Tonya... may I call you Tonya?" Trevor smiled charmingly and continued without awaiting her response. "Did the Sheffields strike you as desperate? Did they lose everything?"

"I'm not sure I can divulge this information," Tonya said, and she felt Patrick grinning next to her.

"The point is, if they have nothing to lose, why wouldn't they join this class-action lawsuit?" Trevor asked.

The food arrived, giving Tonya a moment to think about Trevor's comments.

"We can talk about other things, Tonya. This is complicated legal stuff." Trevor took a bite of his steak. "This steak is excellent."

"Miss Corley is perfectly capable of following this conversation," Patrick said. "Her reluctance to talk stems from not divulging confidential information. Also, she and I have discussed a class action lawsuit, and so far, I don't see the benefit for the clients."

"They'll get money, maybe not as much. But it will be one case. If you handle each case at a time, it will take you years to get through them. How many do you have?" Trevor asked.

"Eleven. I'm fairly confident we can stay on top of them. I don't intend to go out and search for more," Patrick said.

"I think you should think about my offer, Patrick," Trevor said. "It would allow you to search for more cases and get paid even more. It'd be a piece of cake."

Patrick merely grunted in reply.

The three of them ate in silence for a while, and then the conversation drifted to other topics. By the time Tonya had finished her meal, she wondered why Patrick had invited her tonight.

As Trevor got up to leave, he shook Tonya's hand and gave her his business card. "If you ever need *anything*, call me. And even if you don't need a thing, I'd love to see you again. It was a real pleasure meeting you."

"It was nice to meet you, too," Tonya said mechanically.

The men said their goodbyes, and Tonya left the restaurant with Patrick.

"He was nice," Tonya said as she got into the passenger side of Patrick's car.

"Yeah, a real charmer," Patrick said.

He drove in subdued silence for a while, and Tonya wondered what his problem was. Had she said something to annoy him?

"Are you going to call him?" Patrick asked suddenly.

Tonya looked at him in surprise. Were they talking about their personal lives now?

"You don't have to tell me if you don't want to," he said.

"I know," Tonya said. "But I hadn't thought of calling him. I don't need a lawyer."

"I'm pretty sure it's not what he meant. And who can blame him?"

Tonya felt her cheeks get hot. "Not that it's any of your business, but relationships haven't really worked out for me in the past."

Patrick didn't seem to feel rebuffed in the slightest. "What happened?"

Tonya shrugged. "My ex cheated on me."

"What?"

"It's not surprising. Happens all the time," she said.

"To a woman like you? Who in their right mind would cheat on you?" His expression became soft, and he looked at her with concern. "The guy must have been an idiot."

Tonya shrugged. What could say? She had loved him, but he was old news.

A few minutes later, she whispered, "I wonder if he just wanted a way to get out. You know? Get out of marriage and children."

"Still doesn't justify cheating," Patrick said.

She swallowed hard. They were in dangerous territory now. She needed to get this conversation back into professional water.

"Why did you ask me to come to dinner tonight?"

Patrick exhaled deeply. "To be honest, I didn't want to deal with Trevor alone. I can't really stand the guy."

Tonya frowned.

"And I'm glad you came. It was actually quite enjoyable," Patrick said.

He turned into her apartment complex and parked the car.

"Well, here we are." He turned off the ignition.

They looked at each other for a moment.

She was about to say something when her phone rang. It was her mother. She silenced the call and dropped the phone in her purse.

The *Perfect* Plan

Except it didn't land in her purse. It landed somewhere near the cup holders between them.

"I dropped my phone." She cursed under her breath as her hands searched for it.

"No worries. We'll find it," he said.

Tonya unbuckled and bent down to look for her phone. Patrick opened his car door a little, and the interior lights turned on. They looked around the cup holders. Tonya's hands were searching between the seat and the console when she felt his hand touch hers. She looked up and his face was only inches away from hers.

It was as if she was suddenly seeing him for the first time. He was so damn attractive, especially when he wasn't creating silly rules or being rude.

She wondered what it would be like to kiss him. By the look on his face, he thought the same thing. She could feel the heat rising in her cheeks. His eyes were mesmerizing. She could smell his cologne, and suddenly, there were butterflies in her stomach.

A burst of chilly wind blew through the car from the open door, and without a word, the spell was broken. He sat up just as she spied her phone. She hastily grabbed it and stuck it in her purse.

Had they just shared a moment? It looked like he had wanted to kiss her, but he hadn't. Maybe she had imagined it.

She needed to put a barrier between them, just to show him nothing had changed. "Thanks for dinner. I'll see you tomorrow morning, Mr. Rhodes."

His last name worked well, she realized, as he stiffened visibly.

"Goodnight, Miss Corley," he said in his gravelly voice. "Thank you for coming with me tonight."

She nodded and got out of the car and shut the door.

She stood on the sidewalk, staring after him as he reversed the car and sped away. What had just happened between them?

It was bad enough she had a crush on her boss. She couldn't possibly be falling for him, too. And yet, here she was thinking of him long after he had left.

Did he feel the same way?

Chapter 6

TONYA FELT APPREHENSIVE about going to the office the next morning. She had spent too much time thinking about their moment in the car. If she was honest with herself, she had wanted him to kiss her. It was silly, she tried to tell herself. She had kissed other men, and there was never a magic explosion. It wouldn't be any different with Patrick.

Mr. Rhodes. He was Mr. Rhodes to her. Hard to get excited about kissing someone you weren't on a first-name basis with. But still she wondered.

When she walked in, she could hear him on the phone behind the closed door of his office. It was probably for the best. She took a deep breath and buried herself in her current project.

She had made a lot of headway with the Sheffield case. Her research folder on Parachute Executives was growing every day. As complaints mounted against the acquired company, Parachute had shut down operations on Cobblestone Investments. Yet legally they were still liable. She needed all the ammunition she could get for their in-person meeting.

There was a knock on the door, and a young man dressed in fancy slacks walked in.

"Good morning, how can I help you?" Tonya smiled at him.

"I'm here to see Mr. Rhodes."

"Please have a seat." She gestured to the couch. "Can I have your name? Do you have an appointment?"

"Vince Coleman. My appointment's at ten. I'm here a little early though."

"Give me just a moment," Tonya said with a friendly smile.

Her eyes scanned the appointment calendar, and she did a double take. She had scheduled no one for the time slot. Had she made a mistake? Her insides filled with dread. She knew Mr. Rhodes didn't like walk-in appointments. She picked up the phone and dialed his extension.

"I have a Vince Coleman here to see you, but I can't find an appointment for him."

"No problem. Send him in."

Tonya smiled in relief. Finally, he would see clients without an appointment. It just showed people could change, didn't it? As she showed Vince into the lawyer's office, she remembered she hadn't filled out any paperwork for him. What was he even here for?

Mr. Rhodes didn't seem to notice anything amiss. He ignored her and got up to shake Vince's hand.

Tonya closed the door and sat down at her desk. Back to work. There were a few phone calls to handle, and Tonya kept busy taking notes on the Sheffield case.

After the client left, she carefully ventured over to his office and listened at the door. She wasn't interrupting anything. She could just hear the occasional taps on the keyboard. Tonya knocked on the door.

"Come in," Mr. Rhodes said.

Tonya slowly opened the door, and they made eye contact.

"Is this a bad time?" Tonya asked.

"Depends. What do you want?"

The *Perfect* Plan

"I wanted to go over Sabrina's case. I want to start her divorce proceedings, make sure she can get full custody and child support."

Patrick Rhodes shook his head midway through her speech. "I don't have time right now. Get it done and send it to me."

"But..."

"Do you have a specific question? Call me on the phone, and I'll walk you through it. Otherwise, just get it done. Or find someone else who'll do it for free."

"I'll write it up," Tonya said.

"Don't forget the Sheffield case comes first."

Tonya opened her mouth in protest and shut it again. She knew they had agreed for her to do the work on the case, but she had hoped he would take an interest in it, too. She already knew the Sheffield case was more important to him since it might pay the bills, but Sabrina needed their help even more.

Tonya almost slammed his office door behind her in annoyance.

So much for working together on this case.

Just then, a text came through from Daron, asking her out to dinner, as friends. Tonya replied quickly.

I really need to work on my scholarship applications. Maybe another night?

But Daron was persistent.

My extended family runs a scholarship. I can give you the scoop to help you with your application.

Getting the inside scoop on a scholarship was even better than looking for them herself. And after staring at her screen at work all day, she really didn't have the energy to do more of the same at home. She would go to dinner with Daron, she decided spontaneously. There was no reason to sit at home and mope. Besides, it was time for her to concentrate on what mattered most to her. An image of her aunt's blank stare popped into her mind. It was law school she wanted more than anything. And Daron could help her.

Later, when Patrick stepped out of his office to send the last client away, Tonya addressed him deferentially.

"Can I talk to you about the Sheffield matter? I have some documents ready for you to sign."

"Certainly."

Wordlessly, she handed him the printout. She took a sip of her coffee while he read it. The coffee wasn't strong enough, and she made a face.

"This is excellent." He looked at her with appreciation. "You have a way with words."

"What do you want to change?"

He grabbed a pen from her desk and signed his name with a flourish. "Nothing. This is perfect."

He returned the pen, and all Tonya could think about was that he was less than two feet away from her. He was close enough for her to smell his cologne. The same cologne she had smelled on him yesterday when they almost kissed...

"I'm sorry for being short with you earlier. I'm dealing with some family stress," he said.

Tonya hadn't really expected him to apologize. "I understand."

But she didn't fully understand. What was going on with his family? But she wouldn't ask. It wasn't her place.

"Please email me the papers for Sabrina's case. I want her taken care of," Patrick said.

Tonya nodded and smiled in relief.

He seemed to catch her gaze and looked at her for a moment. "You don't like the coffee, do you?"

She tilted her head and said, "I don't know if I would call that stuff coffee."

Patrick laughed, and Tonya tried to focus on her screen again. He still stood unusually close to her desk and looked down at her with that confident smirk she knew so well.

Was he this confident all the time?

The *Perfect* Plan

Why was she having these inappropriate thoughts about him? Was he having them, too? Why was he still standing here?

Tonya asked, "Was there anything else you needed?"

"Need? No," he said. Then he continued in a low voice. "Want? Definitely."

She looked at him in confusion. His eyes were trying to tell her something, but he didn't elaborate. Was he flirting with her?

Before she could figure out what to say, the front door opened. Daron walked in holding a bouquet and wearing a big smile on his face. It was exactly why Daron didn't have a girlfriend. He was trying too hard. Who brought flowers to a dinner date with a friend?

Still, Tonya automatically smiled at Daron before her eyes returned to Patrick's face. He suddenly looked like thunder.

Tonya shut down her computer, grabbed her purse, and walked over to Daron. She wasn't sure if she was happy to see him, but there was probably no woman in the world who didn't enjoy getting picked up by a handsome man holding flowers.

"Thank you. These are lovely." She kissed him on the cheek.

She was about to tell Mr. Rhodes she was leaving when she realized how unnecessary it would be. Obviously, she was leaving, and he was just standing there, watching her, his earlier jovial smile replaced by a deep frown.

Was he mad her friend showed up at work? Did he think Daron was her boyfriend? Did he care? If she was honest, she kind of wanted him to care, at least a little.

"Hello, I'm Daron Faulkner. You must be Mr. Rhodes." Daron stepped over to shake her employer's hand.

Leave it to Daron to make the proper introductions. His parents had raised him right.

"It's nice to meet you."

Despite the casual greeting, her employer's sour expression didn't change. Then she noticed Daron pulling his hand away and shooting daggers at Patrick.

It was definitely time to go. Tonya grabbed Daron's hand and almost dragged him from the building, calling out behind her, "See you tomorrow."

She didn't stick around to hear his answer.

"Your boss squeezed my hand really hard like he was trying to break my bones," Daron complained as soon as the door shut behind them. He examined his hand.

"What?" Tonya was about to chuckle when she caught Daron's expression. "Let's get some ice on it."

"No, it'll be fine. I thought this guy was a lawyer. He should know people get litigious when you crush their hand."

"I'm sorry," Tonya said, only half listening.

Why would Patrick do that? Did Daron's presence bother him? He was almost acting like a jealous boyfriend.

Then she noticed Daron was looking at her and waiting for her to say something. Clearly, he had asked a question. She felt bad for not paying attention.

"What were you saying?" Tonya said apologetically.

He sighed. "Since you weren't listening to me anyway, why don't you tell me what's on your mind?

She blushed. She couldn't possibly tell him she was thinking about her employer's feelings for her.

"Scholarships," she blurted out.

"Have you looked into the Richard Law Scholarship Program? My extended family set this up over a decade ago." Daron pulled out his phone and started typing. "I'll text you the details right now. Consider your problems solved."

They spent a pleasant evening together, eating at a local diner. When Daron walked her back to her car, he hugged her. *Pleasant* described Daron through and through.

"I'll call you," he said.

Tonya nodded and got behind the steering wheel.

Her thoughts drifted to Patrick on the way home. Would a hug from Patrick have been pleasant? Instinct told her no...

At home, Tonya read the instructions for the scholarship program Daron had told her about. She whistled as she took in the information. This was a full-ride scholarship for the handful of people they selected. All she had to do was fill out a questionnaire and write an essay, detailing why she wanted to go to law school. The foundation would then solicit a letter of employment reference from her current employer to complete her application if they selected her. The only snag was the fast approaching deadline.

Tonya immediately opened a new document and started typing furiously.

***

It was the day before they would fly to Savannah. Tonya had been busy tying up loose ends all afternoon. When the last client left, Tonya shut down her computer and collected her things. Patrick stood by the front door, looking through the little window at the top. She wasn't sure if he was looking at anything in particular. Should she wait for him to move to keep her distance?

"How is the family?" she asked him while she slowly made her way toward the door.

He turned around and looked at her. "Fine."

His voice didn't sound as certain and chipper as it normally did, and his face remained stoic.

"You don't sound fine," she said.

That got his attention. His eyes focused on her face now.

"I was just thinking it's a lot easier to represent others and solve their problems than solving one's own problems."

"What's going on with your family?" The words were out of her mouth before she had thought it through. "I mean, you don't have to tell me or anything. It's really none of my business."

But he didn't seem to mind her curiosity. Maybe he was just ready to unburden himself to someone, and she was available to listen.

"Do you have any siblings?" Patrick asked.

Tonya shook her head.

"I have a younger sister. Most of the time, we didn't get along growing up. We were always fighting," he said. "But it all changed when my mother died. Our family has been broken since then. Anyway, my aunt wants us to do something for my sister before she sinks into a depression like our father."

"I never pictured you as the older brother," she said. "But I guess it makes sense."

"What do you mean?"

"I don't know. You always get your way," she said.

"Not always," he said under his breath.

She realized the double meaning of his words immediately. He seemed to have caught it, too. The atmosphere between them changed.

There was an electric charge between them—much like she had felt in the car the other day. His gaze wandered down to her lips. She could almost read his thoughts, and she was pretty certain they mirrored her own.

She could feel her heart beating faster and there was a distinctly nervous and excited feeling in her belly. He was going to kiss her!

As he bent his head down toward her, all she could think about was how much she wanted him to kiss her.

He didn't disappoint. When his lips came down on hers, she realized he kissed with the same intensity he did everything else. She could feel her desire building as his lips explored hers. Tonya couldn't remember the last time someone had kissed her like this. Passionately. She dropped her purse to put her arms around his neck and pulled him closer.

His hands were in her hair, and his thumb was caressing her cheek. She could feel his barely restrained passion as he deepened the kiss. When a moan escaped her lips, he took a step back.

He was breathing hard and so was she. They looked at each other.

He rubbed his chin, "What just happened?"

"You kissed me," Tonya said breathlessly.

"Oh my God." Patrick ran his hands through his hair. "I did. But this can't happen."

Tonya nodded in agreement. It was not a smart idea.

"You're my employee. I don't need a harassment lawsuit." He sounded really worried now.

Was that all he could think about? That she might sue him for this?

Logically, she understood where he was coming from. They were definitely breaking the rules. Still, it stung.

She closed her eyes for a moment. Deep breaths in and out. He still stood there, looking concerned.

She would take the high road. She could not let him see how much this hurt her feelings.

"Calm down. I won't sue you." She said it quietly but with a hint of disdain.

"I appreciate it," he said. "Look, this is just not the time and place. Me and you, we have to keep it professional. You understand, right?"

"Perfectly."

Without saying anything else, she opened the door and left the house.

She wanted to slam the door in frustration, but then he would know she cared.

Cared too much for him. Why did she always choose the wrong guys? First, it was the one who cheated on her and then the one who fell in love with her best friend. And now it had to be the one she worked for?

Her lips still felt like they were burning.

Tonya was practically shaking with nerves when she woke up. She had tried to go to bed early, but sleep proved impossible. Her thoughts kept going back and forth between the kiss and that she was about to fly first class for the first time in her life. And she would travel with Patrick.

How would he treat her after their kiss?

By the time she got to the airport, she was a nervous wreck. As she parked her car, she mentally ran through the list of things she could have possibly forgotten. She hardly paid attention to the attendant who gave her a parking pass. She took the bus to the terminal and pulled out her phone. She had plenty of time to go through security.

Going through airport security with a first-class ticket was a novel experience. The queue was much shorter, and the attendants were nicer than she remembered from her last flight. It had to be chance. Or did they hire different staff to serve first-class travelers? Or maybe they just got paid more?

She was happy to discover a coffee shop on the way to the gate and promptly bought a large latte macchiato. She took a sip and sighed. Everything would be fine. This would be a great day, despite everything.

At the gate, she saw Patrick Rhodes feverishly pecking away on his laptop. It made her heart beat a little faster to see him. She just couldn't get sucked into his gaze this time. She needed to keep her distance.

Even as she got closer, Patrick didn't look up from his screen. Tonya wanted to roll her eyes at him. Did the man ever stop working? She wondered what made him want to earn money so badly. He already lived in a mansion. Maybe he had a huge mortgage to pay.

Why did she even care? It wasn't any of her business.

She sat across from him without saying anything. There was no need to interrupt him. They would have plenty of time to talk later. She looked around the waiting area. Some people were reading books, several business travelers were using computers and phones, and others were just quietly talking to each other. She saw a few families with young children and smiled.

A family was what her mother wanted for her. And maybe someday, she would have one. But maybe not.

"A penny for your thoughts."

She looked up at the sound of his familiar voice. Patrick focused on her face. She hadn't even noticed he had stopped typing. How long had he been watching her?

She would not tell her boss she was daydreaming about having a child one day. Especially not after kissing him the night before.

"Just thinking about the trip. I'm excited to see Savannah."

He nodded slowly, as if he didn't quite believe her. "How's your coffee?"

"I got a latte. It's good." Tonya smiled as she took another sip. Good didn't begin to describe it. There was no better way to start the day.

It didn't take long before they boarded the plane. Tonya had been reading her book when Patrick suddenly packed up his laptop and got up to stretch.

Tonya followed him onto the plane and took her seat at the window. Immediately, a flight attendant offered her a glass of champagne, which she took without thinking.

She turned to Patrick and whispered, "Since when do they serve champagne on the plane?"

"Since always, if you fly first class." He grinned at her.

She blushed. Suddenly, she felt like a child who was pretending to be a grownup. There was an entire world out there she had never experienced, and would probably not experience again soon. She sipped her champagne and smiled. She would take advantage of it while she could.

"What's on the agenda?" Patrick looked at her expectantly with his bright blue eyes, and she realized how close he was sitting to her. This was first class, and the seats were wider than she was accustomed to. But they still shared an armrest, and she could feel his skin on hers.

She wanted him to kiss her again.

Except kissing was not on the agenda, Tonya reminded herself. She moved her arm and tried to think of the day ahead.

"Meeting with Parachute Executives at noon. They didn't tell me how long it would last. It probably depends on whether or not we reach an agreement. We may meet with them again tomorrow morning at eight."

"What exactly did you want to see in Savannah?" he asked.

Tonya looked at him blankly for a moment. Then she remembered their earlier conversation about architecture. He knew she wanted to go sightseeing. And Tonya had spent several hours online trying to decide which places she would like to see, but there were so many to choose from.

"I definitely want to go to Forsyth Park," she began enthusiastically. "I want to go on one of those historic tour buses where they tell you everything about the city. I want to stroll along River Street. There are some House Museums I wanted to see and maybe the Cathedral of St. John the Baptist..."

"Whoa, you know you only have one evening to do all this, don't you?"

Tonya suddenly felt deflated. "I know."

He looked at her for a moment. "I'll tell you what. After the meeting, I'll take you to Forsyth Park, because it's worth seeing."

She looked at him with interest.

"You could just do a bus tour, but it's not exactly tourist season. They may not even be running," he said as he rubbed his chin.

She swallowed as she remembered his hands in her hair. She needed to focus on the conversation.

"I'd love to see Forsyth Park."

"If you're into museums..." Patrick started. "Never mind." He shook his head.

Tonya looked at him curiously. "What were you going to say?"

He seemed lost in thought. Tonya waited, and her patience was rewarded a few minutes later.

"Well, I was thinking we could visit my aunt. She lives in the most beautiful home imaginable, worth all the museums you could visit in Savannah."

She smiled gratefully. "Sounds wonderful. I didn't know your aunt lived in Savannah. Did you grow up there?"

"I know the city pretty well."

He had dodged her question, but still, she couldn't believe her good luck. Tonya was suddenly excited about seeing the house his aunt lived in. Presumably, his entire family lived in mansions, which wouldn't surprise her.

"Thank you for the offer. I'd love to see your aunt's house."

The plane had picked up speed, and Tonya looked out of the window as they lifted off the ground. The view of the city was spectacular. By the time she returned her attention to the cabin, Patrick was working on his laptop again. He was a workaholic. While she would often get to the office early, she knew he worked late every night.

Then again, there wasn't much else to do on the plane but watch a movie or read a book. Tonya unfolded her TV monitor and started browsing through the selection. She selected *My Best Friend's Wedding* to keep herself busy for a while.

As the movie wore on, Tonya remembered why she hadn't watched it in a while. Only one woman could marry the principal character named Michael, and both of them were in love with him. She turned off the TV in annoyance.

"Are you okay?" She hadn't realized Patrick had paid any attention to her.

"Yeah, I'm fine. Just tired of watching," she lied.

"How can you tire of Julia's scheming?" Patrick said with a smile.

"I've already seen it." Tonya felt her voice break a little. She couldn't start crying in front of him about a movie. She wiped her eyes with her sleeves, hoping he hadn't noticed.

"The idea people would do anything for love is interesting," Patrick commented quietly.

She looked at him, and he silently handed her a tissue.

"You probably think I'm silly." Tonya wiped her eyes and took a deep breath, thankful he hadn't made fun of her.

"No," he said. "You're just a romantic."

Tonya blushed. It was a good thing he didn't know she had almost married for money. Although it shouldn't matter what he thought of her. He would not date his employee.

It made her wonder about the woman he had proposed to. Had she worked for him previously? Was she the reason he had those rules in place? She wanted to ask him, but it felt wrong to pry. It was none of her business.

Patrick's eyes turned back to his laptop. Tonya looked out of the window and noticed signs of civilization below. Momentarily, the airplane started its descent.

They landed smoothly and were the first ones off the plane. Another benefit of flying first class.

When they got out in Atlanta, they had to rush through the airport to catch their connecting flight. Their first flight was late. To add insult to injury, Atlanta had such a big airport it took them an hour to get from one end to the other.

On the second flight, they weren't sitting together. Patrick was next to a woman with an infant, and Tonya sat across the aisle next to a burly man who kept his

The *Perfect* Plan

head buried in his book the entire time. When the airplane accelerated, the baby next to Patrick cried.

Tonya kept her eyes on Patrick to see what he would do. He didn't even take his laptop out. Instead, he talked to the mother, who smiled at him despite the inconsolable crying of her child.

Tonya shook her head. Patrick could certainly be charming, but the men she knew didn't enjoy hanging around babies. Apparently, Patrick was different in that regard, too.

Tonya couldn't turn her eyes away. Patrick had been talking to the baby, and now he was expertly holding it and making soothing noises. The baby even stopped crying and watched him intently. Patrick and the woman kept talking to each other.

Maybe they were discussing diapers, Tonya hoped feverishly. How did Patrick know how to calm a baby? She needed to stop obsessing over this.

She grabbed her book out of her purse and opened it. Just this morning, before she boarded the plane, she hadn't been able to put the book down. Now, she couldn't make sense of the words on the page. After reading the same paragraph three times, Tonya closed the book in frustration.

All she could think of was Patrick flirting with the hot momma over there. Tonya glanced their way again. Patrick was bouncing the baby on his lap, and the kid was giggling.

Patrick noticed Tonya's glance and smiled at her.

And then the kid decided it was tired of the trip. Within seconds, Patrick was covered in vomit. Tonya heard the mother apologize profusely as she took the baby from him. To Patrick's credit, he was being a good sport about it.

When Patrick came back from the bathroom, he had removed his jacket and cleaned up the shirt underneath as best as he could. Tonya had to suppress a grin as he walked back to his seat.

After the plane landed, Patrick remained solicitous to the mother and infant. He helped them gather their stuff and even held the baby again while the mother packed up her things.

Tonya left the plane first and waited at the gate for him.

"It looks like the baby really liked you," she said when the woman and her baby were out of sight.

He laughed. "It's a good thing I brought another suit."

His reaction bewildered her. Wasn't he at least a little mad about what just happened?

"The baby really had you fooled, didn't it?"

"It wasn't the first baby to puke on me, and I bet it won't be the last, either," he said as he walked off to the nearest bathroom.

When Patrick emerged in a new suit, Tonya couldn't help but look at him in amazement.

He really seemed to have the whole package. It was so unfair. He was hot. He had offered to be her tour guide when he had no reason to. And he liked babies. It was no wonder she felt drawn to him.

Hoping he couldn't read her mind, she led the way toward the car rental agency. They didn't talk while he signed the paperwork for the car.

When he started the engine, he said, "Savannah is much prettier than its airport. You'll see."

Tonya wasn't quite ready to change the topic. "I didn't know you liked babies."

He weaved skillfully into traffic as he considered his answer. "Babies are cute. So are kittens and puppies. Everyone thinks that."

"Not everyone would willingly play with a stranger's baby."

"Maybe not. I have a large family. My cousins are older than me, and many of them already have kids. I've been around kids my entire life."

Something stirred inside of her. "It was sweet of you to play with her baby."

The *Perfect* Plan

"Taking a baby on an airplane is one of the hardest things anyone can do. That woman deserved a medal," he said.

"She seemed nice."

"I guess. I was just trying to make it easier for her."

"Where's her husband?"

They stopped at a red light, and Patrick looked at Tonya thoughtfully for a long moment.

"What? What's wrong?"

Why was he looking at her like that? Then she realized she was acting like a jealous girlfriend. Very inappropriate. Much like the thoughts she had about him lately.

The light turned green, and he turned his attention back on the road, but the upturned corners of his mouth and gleeful tone of his voice didn't escape her notice.

"Her husband is overseas. She's visiting her parents for a while to have some help with the baby."

"Oh. That must be hard for both of them."

Tonya felt immensely relieved. The woman was married. Patrick would not be meeting her tonight. Then Tonya felt silly. He could date someone else back home. And there was nothing she could do about it.

He brought her back to the present. "Here we go. Are you ready for this meeting?"

"Yes." Tonya nodded. She was ready. She grabbed her folder and opened it, even though she had almost every single one of those documents memorized.

Still, she felt a little nervous about her first big meeting with the lawyers of a big corporation. At least, it would take her mind off Patrick and his unusual liking of infants.

Chapter 7

"WE'RE ABOUT TWO MINUTES AWAY from their corporate headquarters," Patrick said as he turned onto another big street.

Tonya closed the folder on Parachute Executives when she got a text from her mother.

I forgot to tell you. I got some mail for you. Why are you using our address? Your Dad almost used your paperwork to get the fire going.

Tonya cursed under her breath. She had used her parent's address for one of her scholarship applications, because they lived in a different county. According to Tonya's research, the schools tried to distribute their approvals evenly geographically, and she figured it couldn't hurt. How could she have accounted for the fact her parents might burn the paperwork?

She hurriedly texted back. *Please keep it safe for me. I'll come over this weekend.*

"Is everything okay?" Patrick asked.

"Yep," Tonya said without elaborating further.

They had finally reached the offices of Parachute Executives, which were impressive. Maybe not impressive from an architectural point of view; the building was more of an eyesore, being taller than all the rest. However, it showed they had deep pockets. As she looked up from the outside, Tonya imagined anyone with an exterior office would have a breathtaking view of the city.

As they walked in, Tonya noticed the marble floors before her eyes wandered over to tastefully decorated walls and windows. Opulent described this building pretty well. The receptionist welcomed them and gave them directions after calling up to confirm their appointment. Tonya and Patrick rode the elevator to the twelfth floor in silence. She was nervous and unsure of what to expect. She gave Patrick a sideways glance. It wasn't obvious what he was thinking, but he gave her a brief reassuring smile.

A team of lawyers greeted them whose names Tonya immediately forgot. They seemed interchangeable to her, a half a dozen men in black suits and ties, who looked important and probably charged hundreds of dollars an hour to be here. The lead attorney, Jack Hayes, offered beverages, which they declined.

"Patrick and Tonya, if I may call you that. We're pretty informal around here. You can just call me Jack."

Patrick nodded and Tonya smiled at Jack. This could be a lot of fun.

After everyone took their places around the table, Jack Hayes began, "Let me start by saying how sorry I am about what happened to your clients, Mr. and Mrs. Sheffield. Here's our backstory: Parachute Executives recently acquired Cobblestone Investments, assuming it was a squeaky-clean operation. But if you dig deep enough, you'll find a lot of dirt."

Tonya nodded but refrained from commenting.

"We have no interest in getting sued by your client or anyone else." Jack Hayes laughed and the rest of the room politely joined in the joke. "Here's our offer."

Jack tossed a piece of paper to them.

Patrick's eyes slowly scanned the paper as Jack slid another copy toward Tonya.

The paper only listed one number. $200,000.

Patrick looked up, and even though his tone was polite, Tonya knew he was mad. "This is what you're offering my client?"

"I can write you a check for this amount right now to close the matter. I have the authority." Jack nodded, pleased with his generosity.

"It's not even half the money they *invested* with Cobblestone," Patrick said carefully.

"You and I know most cases like this never get resolved. The Sheffields are lucky they're getting anything at all. We're not admitting any liability here."

"Let me get this straight. You're asking me to take this check to the Sheffields and hope they'll be happy about it?"

Jack threw up his hands. "This is what I can do for you right now. It's a hell of a lot better than going to them empty-handed. Besides, you know you're legally required to pass along this offer."

"You have some nerve."

Patrick stood up abruptly and the other lawyers looked at him expectantly. Tonya almost expected an outburst, but Patrick kept his cool.

He held everyone's attention by telling them a story about Mr. and Mrs. Sheffield and how hard they had worked to accumulate those retirement savings. He told them how the elderly couple had come into his office, literally supporting each other, telling him of their misfortune. And he continued with how neither of them had blamed the other for not seeing through the sales rep from Cobblestone Investments. They didn't point fingers in their relationship.

"But I'm pointing a finger today," Patrick continued. "Your company is responsible for the misdeeds of Cobblestone Investments. I don't think you could find a jury in this state who wouldn't find them guilty and award a huge verdict to these retirees. The only drawback to taking this case to a jury is it will take time.

Possibly more time than the Sheffields have left on this Earth, which is precisely why they were targeted."

"It's a beautiful story, and I sure hope no jury will ever hear it," Jack Hayes said.

"A million dollars is what it will take to keep this case away from a jury. A million for the Sheffields, plus lawyer fees. That's our offer," Patrick said.

Jack laughed out loud. "It's ridiculous."

"It's not ridiculous. It's reasonable, considering how much pain and suffering your company has caused my clients."

"I've already made you an offer. That's the best I can do," Jack Hayes said.

"I know it's not your decision to make," Patrick said. "We'll let our clients know about your offer. We're staying in Savannah for the night. Let's talk again in the morning."

Patrick and Tonya rose and shook hands with Jack Hayes and the rest of his legal team.

"Nice job, Patrick," Tonya said as they left the room together.

"What's with the first naming?"

She looked at him mischievously. "I just followed their rules."

He laughed out loud, and she grinned.

"Let's go visit Aunt Mildred," he said as they rode in the elevator.

***

The building that housed Parachute was far behind them when Tonya hung up the phone and took a deep breath.

"What did the Sheffields say?" Patrick asked, without taking his eyes off the road.

"They'll take the money if that's all they can get. But naturally, they had hoped for more," she said.

Patrick nodded.

The *Perfect* Plan

Tonya rolled down her window to take in the sights. As they drove through alley after alley of willow trees, she grinned from ear to ear. She caught sight of several of the beautiful squares the town was known for, and she couldn't even process the number of gorgeous homes she had seen.

When she looked over at Patrick, she noticed he was smiling to himself. Maybe he was inwardly laughing at her, but she didn't care at the moment. The entire world could know she was a tourist here, and it wouldn't have bothered her.

When he finally parked in his aunt's driveway, she stepped out of the car and surveyed the mansion in front of her. It looked just like the home in *Gone with the Wind* minus the plantation part of it, she decided. It had beautiful white columns, big front marble steps, and a balcony, which wrapped around the entire house. The best part was the weeping willow tree in the middle of the front yard. She couldn't wait to get closer and touch the bark to see if maybe these trees had some magic in them.

Maybe she would do it later when nobody was watching.

She turned around to retrieve her purse from the car and almost ran into Patrick. He had come up behind her, lugging her small suitcase and his duffel bag.

"Thanks," she said as she reached awkwardly for the bag.

"I got it. Just go ring the doorbell, will you?"

Tonya did as he asked and trudged up to the house. For the first time she wondered what his Aunt Mildred would be like. She didn't have to wonder for very long.

The door opened, and a little, stout woman stepped out to greet them enthusiastically. "Patrick, it's good to see you."

Patrick put the bags down and bent down to hug her. "Aunt Mildred, this is Tonya Corley."

Tonya extended her hand for a more formal greeting, but Aunt Mildred embraced her in a hug as if she were a long-lost cousin of sorts.

"We don't do formal around here, darlin'. Come on in and get comfortable."

Tonya raised her eyebrows at Patrick, who just shrugged. Relax, she told herself. Just go with the flow.

"Why don't you show her to her room, Patrick?"

"Wait a minute; I thought we were staying at a hotel," Tonya said to Patrick.

It just dawned on her he was bringing in her suitcase, which should have stayed in the car. Her eyes darted between the suitcase, Patrick, and his aunt.

"No, honey. You don't need to stay with strangers. I got plenty of space to keep you comfortable. Patrick will show you."

"That's very kind of you, Ma'am," Tonya said.

"Call me Aunt Mildred, dear. Just go on up and follow Patrick. He'll show you where you can put your things. I don't go up the stairs if I can help it."

Tonya smiled politely at Aunt Mildred and followed Patrick up the staircase. As they reached the top of the landing, she hissed at him.

"You knew we were staying here. You already got the bags out of the car before she even opened the door."

"Relax. This is a beautiful home. You'll get the best room up here. I'll show you."

"What happened to the hotel room?"

"Have you ever heard of Southern hospitality? You can't visit relatives and stay in a hotel room. It's just not how it's done around here," Patrick said.

"They're not my relatives."

"Doesn't matter. You're with me, and therefore, you're our guest." Patrick opened one of the bedroom doors. "Stop pouting and check out this room."

"I wasn't pouting."

"Yes, you were."

Tonya glared at him, but he just grinned at her with a sparkle in his eyes. It was as if this place had transformed him into a different version of himself. Playful. God, he was irresistible when he looked at her this way.

She turned away from him and surveyed the room, trying to collect her thoughts. What she saw took her breath away. At the center of the room was a huge four-poster bed with at least a dozen lacy throw pillows. If she had come here as a child, she would have felt like a princess. The entire room looked as if it could have been part of a castle. The furniture was ornate and vintage, and the carpet plush and soft.

"What do you think?" Patrick watched her reaction closely.

Tonya suddenly felt bad about complaining. This room was much prettier than any hotel room she had ever stayed at. When she walked over to the window, she had an unobstructed view of the willow tree she had admired earlier. She even spied a magnolia tree. She turned around and smiled apologetically at Patrick.

"I take it all back. This is heavenly."

He grinned. "Apology accepted. Make yourself comfortable. The bathroom is right down the hall if you want to freshen up. I'm going to put my stuff in my room. Then we can check out Forsyth Park before it gets dark."

"Thank you," Tonya mumbled.

She had almost said his first name, too. He wasn't Mr. Rhodes to her in this house at all. The entire trip had felt as if she was going on vacation with a friend. A handsome friend.

"You're welcome."

Just as Patrick left the room, a fluffy orange cat squeezed through the door. Patrick seemed excited to see the cat and picked him up. He looked at Tonya with concern.

"You're not allergic to cats, are you?"

"No. I love cats, but my landlord doesn't allow them." She came up next to him and gently petted the cat. "What's his name?"

"Garfield," he said.

She stroked his soft fur and accidentally brushed against Patrick's arm. Her hand hovered in the air for a moment.

"I know he doesn't really look like Garfield, but my Aunt Mildred humored me. She got him when I was a senior in high school. I wanted to take him home, but my mother... Well, we couldn't take him."

She understood immediately why his aunt got him the cat. His mother had just died.

"I'm sorry about your Mom." She avoided his eyes and patted the cat again. "You could take him now," she added gently.

"True. But Aunt Mildred needs him more than I do. He keeps her company when she's lonely. Besides, he's too old to move. He must be like thirteen or fourteen by now."

"He's beautiful," she said.

Her eyes met his, and she felt a spark again between them.

"Do you like dogs?" she asked on a whim.

"I don't mind dogs, but I'm not a dog person if that's what you mean," he said. "Why?"

Tonya shook her head and smiled. "Not important. I was just wondering."

When he closed the door behind him, Tonya exhaled deeply. She had to stop thinking about Patrick this way. She really needed to keep herself in check. She couldn't give in to her desire to play twenty questions with him. He was not some guy she could get romantically involved with. He was her boss, not a potential boyfriend.

Tonya pulled a hairbrush out of her suitcase and tiptoed over to the bathroom. She would make herself look presentable before they headed out again.

The bathroom was just as opulent as her bedroom. Instead of a shower, it held an enormous claw-foot tub.

Tonya walked over to the tub, hairbrush in one hand. She touched the cool, smooth surface with her other hand as she envisioned taking a luxurious bath here. The tub was practically screaming her name, but a bath would have to wait until later.

When she came down the stairs ten minutes later, she overheard Aunt Mildred talking to Patrick.

"I hope you don't stay out too long, Patrick. I'm making dinner." The doorbell rang. "That must be Megan."

"Megan's in town?" Patrick's voice suddenly sounded excited. "It will be nice to see her."

Who was this Megan he was so happy to see?

Tonya heard a joyful shriek and watched a cute brunette run toward Patrick. He hugged her fiercely, and Tonya felt as if she would burst with jealousy. Still, she was careful to keep a smile plastered on her face lest anybody suspected what was going on inside her head.

"Megan, let me introduce you to Tonya Corley."

Tonya stepped down and automatically shook hands with Megan. Megan was beautiful despite the serious expression on her face.

"Tonya, this is my sister, Megan," Patrick said.

His sister! Megan was his sister. Tonya's relief was palpable. And now she could see the similarities between them. Her smile for Megan was now genuine.

"It's nice to meet you," Tonya said.

When Megan didn't respond in kind and turned her attention to her suitcase, Tonya suddenly felt self-conscious. Was Megan being outright rude or was she imagining it?

Tonya looked at Patrick, who was watching her intently. Had he witnessed her reaction to meeting his sister? Tonya knew her emotions always showed plainly in her face for anyone who cared to read them. She felt a little embarrassed, but nothing could dampen her joy now that she didn't have to make small talk to one of Patrick's girlfriends.

"Megan, you can give me a hand, and you two have fun now." Aunt Mildred waved at Patrick, who laughingly opened the front door again.

He smiled brightly when he gestured for Tonya to go first.

An hour later, they were still in the car driving through Savannah. Patrick turned out to be an excellent guide of the city. Tonya listened intently as he pointed out important landmarks to her and explained the history behind them.

"How do you know so much about this city? Did you live here at some point?" Tonya asked.

"For a few months, I stayed with Aunt Mildred and Uncle Morris. Uncle Morris is my grandpa's brother on my dad's side. I lived with them after I graduated high school while I worked on the weekends as a tour guide."

"And here I thought you were just knowledgeable about the city. You're nothing but a show-off."

Patrick grinned, "Fooled you, didn't I?"

She laughed.

"Your aunt is quite the character," Tonya said. "What was her husband like?"

"Uncle Morris was something else. He hated lawyers, for one."

"Surely, he wouldn't have hated you."

"Maybe. Someone scammed him. I was just a kid, and I didn't understand what was going on. I think it was like the Sheffield case. Some guy showed up and promised Uncle Morris big money. He went for it." Patrick shook his head. "He never saw a dime off the 'investment' they sold him."

"That's terrible."

"And nobody would help him. He talked to a lawyer, but the guy wasn't interested. Not sure if Uncle Morris just went to the wrong lawyer. But he gave up. It kind of ruined him, you know. He started drinking…"

"But your aunt and uncle still had this enormous mansion. Surely, it didn't ruin him financially?"

"The house didn't belong to them. Aunt Mildred inherited it from her father just a couple of years ago. That's also who owned the house I currently live and work in. My aunt and uncle were merely scraping by before then. When Uncle Morris died, his life insurance helped turn my aunt into a wealthy woman."

Tonya digested this in silence for a few moments. She had pictured Patrick's family as well-to-do people from the moment she had first asked for an interview. Even though his aunt was a wealthy woman now, Patrick hadn't been raised with a golden spoon in his mouth.

Patrick said dismissively. "Enough of the sob stories. Let me show you the most beautiful place in town."

It took a while for them to find a parking spot, and they walked a few blocks to Forsyth Park. Tonya noticed there were less than two feet between them, but he didn't seem to care. For a moment, it seemed as if he was going to hold her hand, but then he stuck his hands resolutely in his pockets.

By the time they walked up to the fountain, the sun was already setting. Tonya drank in the sight of all the surrounding beauty. When she turned around, she saw Patrick snapping her picture.

"You'll want proof you were here, don't you?"

"I guess," she said uncertainly.

As he took another picture, a stranger approached Patrick. "Do you want me to take a picture of the two of you?"

Tonya put up her hands in refusal. But before she could say anything, Patrick handed the stranger his phone.

"That would be great. Thank you."

A second later, Patrick stood next to her, draping his arm around her. He whispered in her ear, "Smile at the camera."

She smiled as instructed, but her heart was beating so fast she was afraid he could hear it. She tried to tell herself not to be ridiculous. He was just putting his arm around her. It was almost like a hug.

Nothing sexual about a hug.

Except all she could think of was how much she wanted him to keep touching her.

Patrick retrieved his phone and thanked the stranger, and Tonya suddenly felt cold. The wind had picked up, and the sun was disappearing in one last glorious glow of red.

"What was that all about?" Tonya looked at him.

What was going on with him? Why did he suddenly act affectionately around her?

"Nothing," he said, careful to avoid her eyes. "It's the tourist thing to do. Taking pictures in front of the sights."

She frowned. She didn't buy his nonchalance. He had acted differently all day. But if she questioned him further, she might just ruin the mood. It probably had something to do with being home for him.

As they sauntered back to the car, Patrick noticed Tonya was shivering. He took off his jacket and offered it to her. When she shook her head, his voice sounded a little angry.

"Don't be silly. You're cold. It's just a jacket."

"Fine." She relented and put it on. This was much better. "Thanks."

"You're welcome."

They drove back to Aunt Mildred's house in silence. Tonya tried to organize her thoughts, but her feelings got in the way. Wearing his jacket didn't help, because it smelled like him, too. She took it off and handed it back to him before they walked into the house.

As soon as they opened the door, Tonya was hit with the heavy smell of cooking. Her stomach growled, and she took a deep breath.

"What's your aunt making for dinner? It smells amazing."

"She'll have made a feast, I think. Southern hospitality. You couldn't stop her if you tried," Patrick said, visibly proud of his aunt.

Aunt Mildred was excited to have guests. She had set the dining room table with the good silver. There was enough food to feed a family of seven. Fried chicken, homemade cornbread, green beans, okra, and a peach cobbler for dessert. Garfield seemed excited, too. Instead of being asleep on a chair, he sat under the table hoping for scraps. Patrick and Megan didn't disappoint him.

"This was probably the best meal I've ever had," Tonya said after dinner, leaning back in her chair.

Aunt Mildred beamed. "I'm glad you enjoyed it, darlin'. You look like you could use a good meal."

"I've missed your cooking, Auntie," Megan said.

"It was excellent as always, Auntie. Thank you." Patrick walked around the table and bent down to kiss his aunt on the cheek before he carried a pile of dishes to the kitchen.

"It was such a pleasure to cook for y'all," Aunt Mildred said, beaming after him.

They tackled the cleanup together. Tonya was in awe of the elderly woman who moved around the house with grace and speed. She was a big woman, and Tonya couldn't picture her running a marathon, but she seemed to have no trouble doing an endless number of chores in the kitchen. Patrick was at ease here, too. She had never seen him laugh and joke around as much as he did with his aunt and sister.

Just when she thought they would call it a night, his aunt turned on the radio to a country station. As the music filled the kitchen, Patrick bowed to his aunt and extended his hand. She laughed but got up and twirled around the kitchen with him.

"These two," Megan said disapprovingly, but she was smiling. "I'm not much of a dancer, but Patrick has a flair for it."

"How did he learn to dance?" Tonya asked.

"Our mother taught him."

Tonya felt awkward. What could she say to this woman she had never met? *Sorry your mother died?* It didn't seem nearly enough.

But Megan seemed to be in the mood to share. "Our mother passed away when I was thirteen. Patrick was sixteen. We lived with Auntie for a while. It's fortunate she likes to dance, too."

"I didn't realize you were both so young. It must have been rough," Tonya said.

"It was, but it's in the past."

Megan shrugged as if she had lost interest in the matter. Tonya looked at her profile, briefly wondering what was going on in Megan's head.

Then she turned her attention to Patrick and his aunt. Tonya had never seen anyone dance with such gusto. When the song ended, Aunt Mildred sat down breathlessly.

"Your turn, honey. I need to catch my breath," she said to Tonya.

Before she could object, Patrick was pulling her up by the hands.

"I really don't know how to dance," Tonya admitted.

Dancing fell into the range of athletic events she avoided, even though the only risk involved tripping over her own feet.

"Just follow my lead," Patrick said as he twirled her around.

She couldn't help but smile as she stumbled through the kitchen with him. She concentrated on the pressure of his hands and let him guide her. Halfway through the song, she got into the rhythm and beamed at him.

"You're getting it," he said as he smiled at her.

Suddenly, she became aware of how his hands were holding hers. He was close enough to kiss one moment, and the next he twirled her away from him. It suddenly seemed more than a harmless little dance.

Just then, she lost her footing and tripped. She would have hit the kitchen floor if he hadn't caught her in his arms. This was it. She would die of embarrassment in Aunt Mildred's kitchen.

"Are you alright?" Patrick looked at her with concern as his firm hands held her.

"I'm just not good at dancing." Tonya extricated herself from him and sat down shakily.

She wasn't sure what made her feel more flustered, tripping over her own feet or the feel of his hands on her hips as he steadied her.

"It's alright, honey. It's been a long day." Aunt Mildred patted her arm. "Don't compare a beginner's attempt with Patrick here. He's been dancing since before he was out of diapers."

Megan laughed.

Tonya shot Patrick a curious look, but he only shrugged.

"I haven't danced in a while, Aunt Mildred," he said.

"That's a shame. You work too much," she said.

Tonya had to agree with her, although she would never say as much to his aunt.

"Speaking of which, I have some work to do," Patrick said. "Thanks for a lovely dinner and dance." He kissed his aunt on the cheek. His sister got a hug.

"I'll see you in the morning," he said to Tonya.

Tonya nodded and watched him leave. A moment later, she saw Garfield stretch from his place under the table and leisurely go after Patrick.

"The cat drives me crazy," Aunt Mildred said, but her eyes twinkled happily as she watched it disappear.

"He's always liked Patrick more than anyone else," Megan observed dryly.

Tonya looked at Megan with interest. Megan was almost the opposite of Patrick, reserved and bordering on rude. Tonya couldn't quite figure her out.

Aunt Mildred yawned. "Lord, I'm ready for bed. You go on up and make yourself comfortable. Breakfast at seven? Patrick said you have an early meeting tomorrow."

Tonya nodded obediently. "It sounds lovely. Thank you."

"You're welcome, honey." Aunt Mildred turned off the light as the three of them left the kitchen together. "Don't let Patrick fool you, Tonya. He's a good man. He really is."

"He's also a fool about women," Megan mumbled next to her as they listened to Aunt Mildred shut her bedroom door.

"What do you mean?"

Megan shrugged. "I'm sure you've seen the video."

Megan looked at Tonya with shrewd eyes. Tonya nodded slightly. She was dying to ask questions about the woman in the video, but she had a feeling Megan wouldn't be very forthcoming with information.

Megan said, "Then again, he's just your employer, so it doesn't matter to you, does it?"

It was a good thing the room was dark, because Tonya could feel the color rise in her cheeks. She couldn't think of an appropriate reply, either.

She cleared her throat as Megan chuckled.

"I thought there was something between you," Megan said. "If I were you, I'd stay away from Patrick. It just won't end well."

There was a fervent denial on her lips, but Tonya swallowed the words. It didn't even matter if Megan was right or not. She couldn't date her employer.

"Thanks for the advice, I guess," Tonya said, but she knew she sounded hurt.

"I'm sure you know this, but it's not even about you," Megan said.

"It's about the woman who said no to his proposal, isn't it?"

Megan shrugged. "How would you feel if someone publicly stomped on your heart and spread a video of it online?"

"Vindictive, probably."

"Patrick only uses logic. He thinks he can protect himself from letting it happen again by keeping his distance." Megan yawned as if the matter was of supreme indifference to her. "Anyway, you seem nice, and I thought I'd warn you."

Tonya nodded slowly. "I should probably go to bed. Are you sleeping upstairs, too?"

"No. My favorite room was taken when I arrived," Megan said. "There's another guest room downstairs and a separate bathroom."

"Did I take your room? I'm sorry. I didn't even mean to stay here. We had reservations for hotel rooms…"

Megan waved her concerns away. "It's no big deal. This house is well built. I won't be able to hear Auntie or Patrick snore in any of the rooms." Then she added, "Good night, Tonya."

With those parting words, Tonya mounted the stairs. The light was on in Patrick's room, but she didn't peek in on him. She knew he didn't like interruptions when he was at work. At the office, he kept his door shut most of the time, too.

Instead, she went into her room and looked at her surroundings when she remembered the bathtub. A bath was just what she needed after this full day of adventure. She couldn't even remember the last time she had soaked in a tub.

**

She had no idea how long she had been relaxing in the tub, but the water was finally getting cold. It was time to get out. She carefully stepped out and started drying herself. As the water drained, she rubbed her hair dry. She looked in the mirror while she brushed her hair out carefully.

Her clothes were lying on the floor, but she had no plans to put them back on. She would just go to her room and sink into her bed. She wrapped a towel around her and collected her laundry. After a last look around the room, she turned off the light and stepped into the hallway.

Everything was dark. Patrick must have gone to bed already because there was no light shining under any of the bedroom doors. Since Aunt Mildred had her bedroom and bathroom downstairs, she probably hadn't seen the need to put any nightlights on the upstairs floor.

Tonya carefully took a few steps and cursed under her breath as her toes made contact with a dresser. The door to her room was here somewhere, she was sure of it. Her hands felt around for it for a minute until she finally found the door handle.

Relieved, she slowly opened the door and closed it quietly behind her.

Something was off. As her eyes adjusted to the moonlight streaming into the window, she realized her mistake.

"To what do I owe the pleasure of your company?"

She shrieked as she heard his deep voice from the bed and involuntarily dropped her clothes.

"You scared the shit out of me."

"You're the one who showed up in my room unannounced," Patrick said as he slowly got out of bed and walked toward her. "What are you doing here?"

She couldn't help but stare at his muscular chest and arms as he stepped into her line of vision. He was wearing boxers, and there wasn't much left to the imagination. Tonya's heart hammered in her chest as she hastily bent down to pick up her clothes. In the process, her towel came undone. She frantically pulled it together and dropped the clothes again.

"Let me help you." He picked up the pile of clothes and opened the door for her. "Your room is next door in case you forgot."

Her face was probably bright red. Was she bound to embarrass herself in every room of this house?

She stepped into the hall but felt disoriented now. She felt his hand on her arm as he gently guided her to her room. Her skin felt like it was burning from his touch.

He carefully deposited her clothes on the chair by her door and turned on the lamp by her bed.

"Thanks," she said, but her voice sounded shrill in her head.

He nodded and was now staring at her. This time, she recognized the look on his face. She saw desire in his eyes before he looked away, his hand on the door handle.

He cleared his throat. "Good night."

"Patrick?"

He slowly turned around at the sound of his first name.

"Thank you for showing me the city today."

He nodded without taking his eyes off her. He was breathing a little harder now. She took a step toward him, her feet propelling her forward almost involuntarily.

She wanted to reach out and touch him. He seemed to read her mind as his gaze dropped to her chest where the towel wasn't doing the best job of covering her cleavage.

"You're welcome." His voice sounded deep and gravelly.

She was definitely in trouble if just hearing him talk made her feel this way. They were only inches apart now, and all that stood between them was the cottony fabric around her chest. Patrick's fingers gently brushed her upper arm, and she shivered.

Tonya slowly dropped her towel, purposefully this time, until she stood naked before him.

His voice sounded hoarse when he asked, "What the hell are you doing?"

Instead of answering him, she put her arms around his neck and kissed him slowly on the mouth. Almost immediately, she felt his arms around her as he pressed her against his body and moaned. There was no turning back now.

Not that she wanted to.

He deepened his kiss and explored her mouth skillfully with his. Her knees felt weak as his hands gently cupped her buttocks.

"Are we really doing this?" he said.

Instead of replying, she gently bit his lip and moved her hands down his abs.

He groaned, "I'm not a saint, Tonya."

His use of her first name gave her goosebumps.

She heard him shut the door with his foot, and then there was the quiet click of a door lock being turned. Her nipples hardened as her body rubbed against his. She wanted more. Before she could voice her thoughts, he picked her up and gently deposited her on the bed.

Patrick kissed her with an intensity that took her breath away. He slowly trailed kisses down her neck. Then he took her nipple in his mouth while his hand explored her body. She squirmed when he found her sensitive spot and skillfully massaged it. She whispered his name and ran her fingers along his muscular arms. Her hands grabbed his tousled hair just as she felt him trail kisses along her chest to the other breast. His finger was still inside her, making her ache for more.

She ran her hands down his body and felt him tense up as she reached inside his boxers. She pulled them off and gently ran her fingers up and down his shaft. His lips found hers again, and his tongue tasted hers. She moaned and pulled him on top of her. When he entered her, she inhaled sharply. She had not expected it to feel this good.

Patrick's hand gently touched her face as he kissed her lips and asked, "Are you okay?"

She nodded and pulled him toward her. As they found their rhythm, his lips found hers again.

"I've wanted you for so long," he said between kisses.

She was coming undone underneath him as he continued to pleasure her with long strokes. She reached her climax just before he did.

The *Perfect* Plan

As they caught their breath, Tonya's mind cleared, and she felt mortified for a moment. What had they done? Looking at him, he didn't seem to have a care in the world. Patrick was content to stay with her, and she wasn't ready to end whatever this was.

Nothing. It was nothing. Just a little vacation flirt, she decided, as she drifted off to sleep with him.

During the night, she woke up from his touch. She was nestled in his arms, and he was slowly stroking her back. When she looked up at his eyes, she wasn't sure what he was thinking. There was desire, but there was something else, too.

Maybe doubt about what he was doing here. But she didn't want to spoil it. Not yet. She rolled on top of him and bent down to kiss him, slowly.

"I heard the house is soundproof," she said.

He chuckled. "Is that why you came into my room?"

His hands were on her breasts as she trailed her fingers down his chest.

"No," she said honestly. "It was entirely accidental."

"I'm glad you did," he said. "I heard you run the water in the bathroom." His fingers found her again, and she moaned. "I wanted to join you in the tub."

He continued pleasuring her manually even as he entered her. She arched her back and rode out the waves, reaching a state of bliss just before him.

He hugged her to his chest and gently brushed her hair aside. He kissed her forehead, her nose, and her mouth as she lay there. Exhaustion overcame both of them, and the last thing she remembered was the feel of him beneath her.

In her dreams, she heard her phone ring. The noise stopped before she could wake up enough to find it. Maybe it was all a dream. Her hands found Patrick again, and she snuggled against him, content.

She wasn't dreaming. He was right there with her.

Chapter 8

WHEN TONYA WOKE UP in the morning, sunlight streamed in through the window. She yawned and stretched and reached over to the other side of the bed. Her hands touched cold sheets. Patrick was gone.

She sat up, suddenly wide awake, blushing at the memory of last night. She didn't know what had come over her. Maybe it was seeing him half-naked. Maybe it was dancing with him. Maybe it was listening to his sister's warnings.

If she was honest with herself, she had felt something for him before their first kiss. She was falling for her employer, of all people.

Unfortunately, in broad daylight, having sex with her boss looked like a terrible idea. Maybe he wasn't even too particular about who he went to bed with, as long as a woman offered herself to him.

Which Tonya had done.

But what if he wanted to fire her now? He wouldn't, she decided. At least not while he was still in violation of local zoning laws. By now, she had hoped he would appreciate her work ethic too much to let her go. Except now she had messed it all up by sleeping with him. She felt like such an idiot. What time was it anyway?

She needed to talk to Patrick to figure out what was going on between them. Did last night mean they were dating now, despite his rules? Obviously, he desired her.

Tonya smiled at the memory of his body on hers. It had been more than just sex for her. Maybe he felt something for her, too?

She was suddenly filled with hope and hurriedly got ready for the day.

When she emerged downstairs, she saw the spread Aunt Mildred had laid out in the kitchen. Megan sat at the table, buttering a piece of toast. No Patrick in sight.

Tonya soaked in the smell and smiled in appreciation. There were eggs, bacon, hash browns, and even grits.

"Good morning, Tonya. I hope you're hungry," Aunt Mildred said.

"I am, but it looks like you made enough to feed an army." Tonya smiled at Aunt Mildred. What a sweet soul she was. "You didn't have to go through all this trouble."

"It's no trouble. I enjoy cooking. Patrick already had breakfast earlier. He's upstairs working on some case, he told me."

Tonya's heart sank a little. He was avoiding her. Tonya noticed Megan watching her closely. She forced herself to smile. She couldn't worry about it now, not with his sister watching her.

"I hope you slept well," Megan said.

Tonya nodded, but couldn't trust herself to answer. Did Megan suspect something was up? Surely not. Aunt Mildred added a generous helping of everything to her own plate and did the same for Tonya.

Tonya waited until Aunt Mildred had tried a bite of food before she started eating herself. The eggs were hot, and the crispy bacon was delicious.

"When will I meet this guy, Megan?" Aunt Mildred asked.

Tonya noticed Megan was scowling at her aunt now.

"Probably never. He won't stick around," Megan said defiantly as she bit into her toast.

The *Perfect* Plan

"Megan, honey, I wish you'd give someone a chance."

"I'm not interested. I don't need a man to make it. What do you think, Tonya?"

Tonya's cheeks flushed.

"Don't involve her in our squabbles," Aunt Mildred admonished her niece.

"Why not? Tonya, do you believe in love? Aunt Mildred keeps hounding me to find the right man while I insist it's no use."

"It's a tough question," Tonya stalled. "I like the idea of finding the one, but it's a lot harder than it sounds."

"Precisely my point." Megan nodded approvingly.

"We both know that's not your point at all, Megan. Falling in love means opening yourself up to getting hurt. And you don't dare to do it. It has nothing to do with not being able to find the right man." Aunt Mildred's voice was kind but firm.

Megan was silent.

Tonya stared at the two of them in disbelief. She felt out of place and wondered if she should leave. The conversation seemed to have gotten entirely too personal.

"You're wrong, Auntie. There's just no one out there who's right for me," Megan asserted. "Besides, Patrick's doing the same thing."

Who was she kidding? Tonya wasn't going anywhere if she could learn something new about Patrick and his odd family. She took another bite as she listened intently.

Aunt Mildred touched Megan's hand. "Patrick is different. He just needs time. He'll risk his heart again. And I bet there is a right guy for you out there. In fact, I'll put my money where my mouth is."

"What do you mean?" Megan put the last bite of egg into her mouth and took a sip of water.

"I think given the right incentives, you'd try harder. If you had a nice pile of cash waiting for you as a reward, you'd find Mr. Right in a heartbeat." Aunt Mildred's eyes sparkled.

Megan laughed out loud. She walked around the table and kissed her aunt on the cheek. "You're sweet."

"I just believe men and women shouldn't be alone," Aunt Mildred said primly.

Megan rolled her eyes at her aunt, but she was smiling now. "Thank you for breakfast."

"Think it over, dear." Aunt Mildred called after Megan as she left the kitchen. Then she turned her attention to Tonya. "That girl is really something, but we'll get her hitched all the same."

Tonya smiled uncertainly and finished her breakfast.

After cleaning up the kitchen with Aunt Mildred, Tonya went upstairs to brush her teeth and pack her things. Just as she had zipped up her little suitcase, she heard Patrick's voice in the hallway.

"Are you ready?"

She turned to look at him and smiled shyly. He was wearing a black suit and tie, looking just as handsome as ever. Her thoughts drifted to what he looked like underneath his clothes and how his body had felt under hers last night, and she felt herself grinning.

He avoided her gaze and mumbled, "It's time to go."

"I'm ready," she said.

She heaved the suitcase off the bed and rolled it into the hallway where Patrick took it from her. He was definitely the gentleman his aunt approved of.

But he was careful to keep his distance from her when all she wanted was for him to acknowledge something had happened between them. Why didn't he give her a smile, a look, or better yet, a kiss?

Maybe he had already gotten what he wanted from her. Tonya suddenly felt sick to her stomach.

They said their goodbyes to Aunt Mildred, who hugged them both fiercely. Patrick hugged his sister goodbye, and Tonya awkwardly shook hands with Megan.

Tonya waved half-heartedly as they got in the car. Patrick turned on the ignition while she struggled with her seat belt. They drove in uncomfortable silence for ten minutes. A few times, she tried to say something, but she couldn't come up with a coherent sentence.

Finally, she decided they would have to address the elephant in the room. She couldn't risk losing her job over this. Clearly, he wasn't interested in her anymore. He wasn't even looking at her. She cleared her throat.

"Look... about last night," Tonya started, unsure of how to finish.

"I'm sorry about what happened," he said readily. "It was a huge mistake."

Tonya nodded, silently seething. A *huge* mistake? He had some nerve.

"I was hoping we could just kind of move on and forget about it for now," he said.

"Yeah. Just what I was going to suggest," she lied. Her voice sounded cheery even though she felt like crying and screaming at him.

How could he suggest she forget about it? This must be a typical guy thing she wasn't capable of.

That was not a night she was going to forget. She would have to be careful around him. Surely, it would be easier back at the office. There was the two-foot rule. He would keep his distance.

"What's on the agenda for this meeting?" Patrick deftly changed the subject.

She winced at being reminded of their roles. He was still her employer. He had made his intentions clear enough. He wasn't even remotely interested in a relationship.

Megan hadn't lied about that.

Reluctantly, Tonya pulled out her folder and opened it to the notes from the previous meeting.

Twenty minutes later, they pulled into the parking lot of Parachute Executives and rode the elevator in silence. Something in the atmosphere had changed. They entered the same conference room they had used yesterday, and Jack Hayes greeted them with a smile and a welcoming handshake.

"Thanks for coming back today. I hope you had a good time in Savannah," Jack smiled, trying to lighten the mood.

Tonya smiled graciously and briefly gushed about the city while Patrick's face remained stoic. He was not up for small talk. And apparently, he didn't find Savannah as memorable as she did.

Jack Hayes moved the agenda along. "We discussed your case yesterday afternoon. We know your clients have been through a lot, and they deserve some justice."

Tonya saw Patrick nodding along beside her. So far, Jack had said nothing new, but hopefully, he was on the right track.

"There's a contract, signed by both Mr. and Mrs. Sheffield. In this contract, it states Cobblestone Investment will not assume any market risk as there are no guarantees," Jack said.

"We're talking about theft, not market risk. You and I both know the wording in the contract doesn't give them the right to make off with my clients' retirement fund," Patrick said sharply.

Jack Hayes nodded eagerly, and continued undaunted, "Circumstances being what they are, we have spoken with everyone involved with this case. Mr. Bassett, the vice president of Parachute Executives, stayed late last night to discuss the situation. Together, we've decided to increase our initial offer by fifty percent."

Tonya did a quick calculation in her head. They were now offering $300,000. The Sheffields would receive $225,000 after lawyer fees.

"It's not even close to what the Sheffields have lost," Patrick said. "After lawyer fees, the Sheffields would receive less than half of what they invested with Cobblestone Investments. That's not much of an offer."

"With all due respect, three hundred thousand dollars is a lot of money, Patrick. We have worked hard to agree to this kind of sum. It's a substantial settlement offer."

The *Perfect* Plan

Tonya looked at Patrick. His face was unreadable. She was afraid hers showed openly how she felt about their generous offer.

"I'm not sure we'll come to an agreement today, starting with these numbers," Patrick stated.

"We are trying to meet your demands, Patrick, but you have to admit you're starting much too high." Jack Hayes got up and took a few steps. "I suggest you meet with your clients and lay out the case as it stands. Present our offer to them and let them know we're putting serious money on the table here. But this offer won't last forever. They need to decide."

"Then I suggest you do the same. I'll pass along your offer, and you can sit down with Mr. Bassett and whoever else needs to be there and think about these retirees. They have worked for decades to build up a retirement fund and now have to be happy to have less than half of it returned to them? It boggles the mind." Patrick stood up and straightened his tie. "I'd love to take this case to a jury."

"I don't doubt it." Jack smirked at Tonya, who wasn't quite sure what to do with the gesture. Did he think she was on his side?

She looked at Patrick. He wasn't rushing off. Instead, he waved Jack aside for a private conversation. Tonya knew he would get the best outcome for his clients. She was sure of it.

Within minutes, there were handshakes all around, and a secretary escorted them out of the building.

Patrick and Tonya didn't discuss the case on the way to the airport. Patrick only exchanged a few necessary words with her about where they were going and whether they should get lunch.

She wanted to grab him by the tie and shake him, but that would have been highly unprofessional. He had already made it perfectly clear their relationship needed to stay within the boundaries they had first established.

It was Mr. Rhodes and Miss Corley. Two feet apart.

On the airplane, Tonya closed her eyes to avoid having to look at him or talk to him. The change in air pressure woke her up. When she looked around in a daze, she saw Patrick staring into space. He looked a little sad. When he noticed she was awake, his facial expression became inscrutable.

"Did you sleep well?" he asked.

She nodded and turned her head away. She gazed out of the window without really seeing anything at first. It was dark outside, but the city was lit up. Several stores were already putting up Christmas decorations, even though Halloween was still a few days away.

When they stepped out of the airport an hour later, Tonya took a deep breath. The air smelled fresh, like after a big rainstorm. It was the end of a nice fall day in Texas.

"See you at work tomorrow," Tonya said, waving goodbye to Patrick.

"Okay..." He looked at her intensely, as if he wanted to say something to her.

"Was there anything else?"

"Not really. It's just... It's bad timing," he explained.

Bad timing. She knew immediately he was talking about them, even though she didn't understand what he meant. She shrugged. He didn't need to know how much it affected her.

She grabbed her suitcase and resolutely walked to her car without looking back.

***

When Tonya awoke on Saturday morning, she lingered in bed for a while. Her mind replayed the trip to Savannah more times than she could count. But nothing could change the ending. Patrick wasn't interested in her.

It hurt more than Mark's rejection of her in front of her family. She cared about Patrick, even if she didn't want to admit it. But it would go no further between the two of them.

It was time to recommit to her original goal. Law school. She would get into law school, even if it was the only thing she accomplished in the next year.

But first, she had some catching up to do.

She dove into Sabrina's paperwork. It wasn't difficult to argue for full custody for a woman whose husband had physically abused her and her child. Tonya could barely conceal her hatred for men like Sabrina's husband in the verbiage. At least, she had the medical and police records to prove the abuse. She emailed the file to Patrick for his approval.

If only she could have done the same for her aunt. But she couldn't help someone who didn't want her help.

She refilled her coffee cup and meticulously filled out six different scholarship applications. It was already late afternoon by the time she finally closed her laptop. She stood up to stretch her limbs just as the phone rang.

It was her mother.

"I just wanted to make sure you made it home in one piece from your trip," her mother said.

Almost. Unbidden, an image came to her. The look on Patrick's face when he had told her the timing was off. She still felt wounded. It didn't even compare to discovering Nick with the cheerleader. But it wasn't something she could tell her mother.

"I'm fine, Mom. Airplanes are not scary." She tried to sound breezy as she blinked hard. She would not cry about her employer.

"Well, it wouldn't have hurt you to call when you got back. Your father and I worry about you."

"Thanks, Mom," Tonya said, suddenly grateful to have a mother who could call her. Unlike Patrick, who had been motherless for years.

Why did everything make her think of Patrick?

The conversation drifted to casual topics, and eventually Tonya hung up, not before promising to come over for brunch soon. Just as she sat back on the couch, her phone beeped.

A text message from Victoria. *Hi friend, hope you're doing well.*

Tonya answered. *Just got back from a business trip to Savannah. With my boss.*

Tonya relaxed into the pillow as she waited for her friend's response.

The lawyer? Anything going on between the two of you?

She contemplated Victoria's loaded question, and she suddenly wanted to unburden herself to someone. Who better to tell than your best friend?

We had sex on the trip. And afterward, he blew me off, saying the timing wasn't right. What have I done? How do I fix this?

Victoria's answer came swiftly.

Depends on what you want. If you're still looking for Mr. Right, keep looking. If the lawyer might be Mr. Right, you're in trouble.

Tonya shook her head. She didn't know what she wanted, did she? And she had no idea if Patrick Rhodes was Mr. Right, did she? And even if he was, he had made it abundantly clear nothing else would happen between them.

She sighed and put her phone down. This couldn't be solved by texting anyone.

The phone beeped again. Tonya picked it up. Maybe Victoria had a brilliant idea after all?

But it wasn't her this time. It was an email from Patrick. Tonya clicked on it with shaking hands. What could he be emailing her for?

When she saw the email, she didn't know which emotion to feel. Patrick had signed and scanned Sabrina's paperwork for her to file, even though she had just sent it to him this morning. He was working this weekend on a pro bono case because she had asked him to.

Tonya opened her text messages to Victoria again and typed.
I think I'm in trouble.

***

It hardly seemed fair she had to work for a man who had slept with her and now pretended nothing had happened between them. Tonya briefly thought about quitting on the spot as she got ready on Monday morning. Anything was better than the humiliation of seeing him every day after his blatant rejection of her.

The logical side of her won out. She needed this job to pay the bills until she could get a scholarship. There was no other way around it. Maybe it wouldn't be so bad. Maybe he would just hide in his office.

No such luck for her.

"What's on the agenda this morning?" Patrick was already waiting for her when she opened the door to the office.

Tonya was startled to find him in her space and skirted around him to get to her desk. She took a deep breath and tried to think while her computer booted up.

"Maybe this will help." He handed her a coffee cup.

She took a sip absentmindedly.

Then she looked up at him in surprise. "This isn't coffee."

"Latte macchiato." He grinned.

She smiled. It was nice of him to remember. Her eyes darted over to the coffeemaker. How did he make a latte come out of that thing?

"I bought a new coffeemaker." He seemed to know just what she was thinking.

"Right. Nice. Thank you."

"You're welcome," he said, pleased with himself.

Tonya logged on to her computer and pulled up the calendar.

"We're meeting with the Sheffields today to talk to them about their options. We have to present the offer from Parachutes."

He nodded. "I still don't like it."

"It's their money and their decision," Tonya said firmly.

An hour later, the Sheffields were sitting on the couch in the waiting room. When Tonya told Patrick of their arrival, he promptly rolled his office chair into the bigger room.

When Tonya shot him a confused look, he whispered, "They have a hard time getting up, and I want you to be there, too."

Mr. and Mrs. Sheffield were sitting on the couch, looking at both of them expectantly. After Patrick shook their hands, Mr. Sheffield's hand found that of his wife's. Tonya noticed how she squeezed his hand and interlaced her fingers with his. The tender gesture almost made Tonya cry. She definitely had a soft spot for this couple.

Patrick had rolled Tonya's chair out in front of the couch, allowing both of them to face the Sheffields to tell them what was going on. Tonya was glad she was part of the case, but she was sad she didn't have better news for them.

"There has been some progress on your case," Patrick began. "As you know, we're dealing with Parachute Executives, the company that bought out Cobblestone Investments. We met with their in-house lawyers two days ago. They haven't admitted to anything in writing. However, they've made a second offer we're required to pass along to you. They're willing to write a check payable to the two of you for $300,000 if you drop the lawsuit."

"I don't understand. How is it fair for them to only give us some of our money back and keep the rest?" Mr. Sheffield frowned.

"It's not fair. When big companies get sued, they often like to settle out of court. It means they'd rather pay you money now to make the problem go away than risk the case in front of a jury down the road," Tonya explained. "However, the sum they're offering amounts to less than half of what you lost when you add in lawyer fees."

"How much would we get?" Mrs. Sheffield turned her piercing blue eyes on Tonya.

"When all is said and done, you'll have $225,000."

Tonya had done the math many times already, and it embarrassed her Patrick would take such a sizeable chunk. Not that she blamed him. This battle was far from over, and both of them had already worked for many hours on this case.

"And we could get this money how soon?" Mr. Sheffield coughed a little.

Patrick Rhodes glanced at Tonya before he turned to his clients. "You could have the money a week from signing the papers."

"You're not suggesting we take the offer, are you?" Mrs. Sheffield looked at Patrick. "What else can we do? What are our other options here, Mr. Rhodes?"

"This case could be huge. Parachute Executives doesn't want the terrible publicity a trial would bring. I think they want to settle this out of court, and quickly. A big trial would hurt them. I would like to see them being held responsible for their actions. Unfortunately, court cases and trials take time. It could be several years before we see a courtroom. Until then, no money will change hands. And even after a verdict, they can still appeal the case."

"Pursuing a settlement is not a bad strategy," Tonya said.

"Is this all they'll give us?" Mr. Sheffield asked, not letting go of his wife's hand.

"I don't know what their maximum offer is. We'll continue to work on the negotiations on your behalf," Patrick said.

Mrs. Sheffield nodded. "It seems like a reasonable thing to do."

"What if we can't agree?" Mr. Sheffield asked.

"Until you sign the settlement, we can take the case to court. The potential court case looming over the company makes Parachute Executives push hard for a settlement," Patrick said.

"We have bills to pay..." Mr. Sheffield's voice trailed off.

Tonya remembered their hospitality despite their financial circumstances. "This is just terrible."

"Dear, it's not a big deal. It's just money." Mrs. Sheffield looked at Tonya kindly. "You're young. When you've lived as long as we have, you'll realize money can't buy everything. Besides, we still have each other." And she patted her husband's hand, who smiled at her.

Tonya glanced in Patrick's direction. He seemed lost in his own thoughts, but when he noticed her eyes on him, he raised his eyebrows. What was the man thinking? Tonya averted her eyes and helped the Sheffields gather their belongings.

After the couple left the office, Patrick walked around the room. Tonya moved the chairs back in place, trying to keep out of his way, but he didn't even seem to notice her presence. She left him alone in his current mood and worked on the next letter to Parachute Executives. She typed for several minutes before he started talking to her.

"I wanted to take this case to court. This could have been the break-through point for my career," Patrick said.

"If you want to make a name for yourself, file a class action lawsuit with Trevor." Tonya continued to pound the keyboard.

"What do you mean? Have you been talking to Trevor?"

Tonya almost smiled when she noticed his grim expression.

"I'm just trying to help." Tonya stopped typing. "Look, you're doing the right thing for the Sheffields. Word will spread. And Cobblestone has closed up shop. They're not harming anyone else."

He nodded vigorously. "You're right. Of course, you're right."

"Naturally, I'm right. I work for a lawyer."

His mouth turned up at the corners. "It's pretty rare to see a happy couple who has been married as long as the Sheffields have been."

Tonya turned her chair toward him. "My grandparents are still married."

"Are they happy together?"

Tonya thought of her grandparents and how they had always presented a united front. "I think so."

"What about your parents?" he asked.

Tonya nodded. "My parents are still married. What about yours?" The question came out automatically before she could think it through.

When she saw Patrick's raised eyebrows, she remembered.

"I'm sorry. I didn't think…" Tonya closed her eyes. She had put her foot in it big time.

"It's fine." Patrick took a deep breath.

She looked at him with compassion.

"My father has never gotten over her," Patrick confessed. "He has never even dated anyone since my mom passed away."

"It's sweet your Dad hasn't remarried. There's something to be said about being married to the one person you're supposed to be with. I like the idea."

Tonya sighed quietly. She couldn't even make it to the I-do-part of the ceremony. She wanted to laugh at herself, but it made her feel like a failure.

She blinked back her tears. She would not start crying about her personal life at work. In front of him.

By the time she looked up again, Patrick had quietly shut his office door behind him.

***

"I'm glad you've finally found some spare time for your mother."

Tonya took a deep breath. She hated being treated like a child. No wonder she never visited her parents.

Tonya and her mother sat on the couch in the living room while her father lounged in his recliner, eyes on the football game. Tonya tried to enjoy her coffee over the noise of the TV while her mother delicately picked at the muffin in front of her.

"Have a muffin, Tonya."

"No, thank you. I'm not hungry right now."

It wasn't entirely true. She had already eaten a muffin earlier, and she couldn't justify having another one. Her mother's baking was mostly a curse. It was sheer torture and a strenuous exercise in willpower to resist slices of heavenly carbs. Another reason not to visit every weekend.

"I've been busy with work. We have a big case. I think I told you about it."

Tonya had told her mother about her job. She had been so excited to go to Savannah, too.

"That lawyer of yours is taking advantage of you."

He was not taking advantage of her as much as she wanted him to. He had barely even talked to her since they got back. She shook off the thoughts. Her mother hadn't meant it that way.

And she had tried to banish Patrick from her mind, but seeing him reminded her she still cared about him. She would have to quit her job if she wanted to forget about him. It was a huge predicament to be in.

"How is Daron? His Mom keeps asking when he'll bring you home."

"Oh. Daron is nice, but we're just friends." Daron was nice. Just nice. And Tonya had no desire to meet his mother at all.

The *Perfect* Plan

"I thought I would be a grandma by now. Milly already has three grandchildren." Darlene Corley shot a meaningful glance at her daughter.

"Not all women have kids, Mom."

Despite what she told her mother, Tonya had never pictured herself to be one of these childless women. She had always pictured herself as a married woman this time in her life, and at least planning to get pregnant. But she still had a career to think of. She didn't need a man in her life to be happy.

"What are you going to do with your life then?"

"I'm going to law school next fall," Tonya said.

"You're not getting any younger, you know. I heard thirty-five is considered advanced maternal age."

"I'm not thirty-five for five more years. Besides, I'm happy with my job. I enjoy working on these cases. And I want to make a career out of this." When she noticed her mother's sad expression, she softened a little. "Look, I tried getting married, and the guy left me at the altar for someone else. Maybe there isn't a Mr. Right for everyone."

"That's nonsense, Tonya. And anyway, you don't need to find a Mr. Right. Just find a Mr. who will make you his Mrs." Darlene rolled her eyes.

"You were in love with Daddy, weren't you?"

"When we were younger, yes. We were madly in love. But marriage is different, isn't it, Nicolas?"

"Sure, darling," Nicolas Corley said without taking his eyes off the game.

Tonya grinned. Her parents were really something. Her dad never even paid attention to her mom these days. But maybe that was just what love turned into after a certain amount of time has passed.

The Sheffields were the exception. Their love had lasted. Tonya knew they loved each other, maybe even more than a young newlywed couple. Their love had substance behind it.

"Maybe true love lasts a lifetime," Tonya wondered out loud.

Her mother wasn't listening. She had veered to a different subject. "If you're working hard, your lawyer must be ambitious."

"He is. He's trying to grow his practice."

"All lawyers are greedy and like money."

"That's just a cliché," Tonya said.

"Clichés are often true."

Tonya sighed and took another sip of her coffee. She glanced at her watch. It had only been twenty minutes, but it already felt like hours had passed since she walked through the front door.

Then she remembered Megan and Patrick didn't get the chance to spend time with their mother at all. And she suddenly felt guilty for wanting to leave. Maybe she should make the best of being here.

"Mom, will you teach me how to make those muffins you brought to my house the other day?"

"Sure." Darlene Corley narrowed her eyes. "But since when do you bake?"

"Since today." Tonya smiled. "Come on, Mom. It'll be fun."

And it was fun, Tonya admitted to herself when she got home in the evening. Darlene Corley was in her element in the kitchen. She had never had such a good time with her mother before. Why had she never baked with her before?

Chapter 9

"CHECK OUT WHAT THE courier pigeons brought last night." Patrick Rhodes tossed a letter on her desk.

Tonya perused it, and her eyes widened. It was a letter from the Richard Law Scholarship Program. She jumped for joy and shrieked excitedly. This was it. Her dreams were coming true. All they needed was a reference from her current employer.

Her thoughts returned to the present, and she saw the amused look on his face.

"This is huge," she explained. "I applied for this scholarship a few weeks ago. It's a full ride, and they only ask for employment references as the last check in the box. It means I'm in the running for it."

"Nice." He smiled. "Why didn't you tell me you were applying for law school?"

She shrugged. If she had told him on the first day, he wouldn't have hired her. And even now, things could still go wrong. She might not get the scholarship.

"It sounds like we have a reason to celebrate," he said.

"Well, it's not official yet," she hedged. She hadn't planned on celebrating anything with him, but it would be rude to say it out loud.

"That reminds me. I won't be in the office tomorrow, remember?" she said. "I'll be meeting with the scholarship committee in the morning."

He already knew this, of course. She had asked for a personal day last week, which he had readily granted. Now he knew why she had requested time off. Not that he seemed to care.

"Right," he said before he returned to his office without another glance in her direction.

He could have wished her good luck.

When it was time to leave the office ten minutes later, she slammed the front door behind her for good measure, but it didn't really make her feel any better. It was torture to see him every day, knowing how intimate they had been. And yet, he didn't seem to care about her at all.

Was she feeling heartbroken? Maybe it was just hurt pride. Rejection stung.

But this was nothing like the time Mark had left her at the altar. It had stung, too, but she had bounced right back. By now, Tonya knew it was more than a crush she had on her employer. He was smart, kind, and they had shared an incredible night together.

None of it mattered. He wasn't interested in her.

***

Tonya had originally planned to see her mother after her meeting with the scholarship committee, but she couldn't bring herself to go there on her only day off. Instead, she contemplated what her future would look like. With the scholarship in hand, she would soon quit her job and go to law school full time.

How could she be anything but ecstatic about her dreams coming true?

Instead, she sat at home wondering what Patrick was doing. If she was honest with herself, she already missed him even though she was just taking one day off. How could she live without seeing him every day?

Tonya picked up the phone and dialed Victoria's number. Victoria picked up on the first ring.

"Hi Tonya, what's up?"

"I'm on track to get a full ride to law school," Tonya said.

"Congratulations," Victoria cheered.

"Yeah, it's pretty cool," Tonya said.

"Pretty cool? Why don't you sound more excited about it?" When Tonya didn't answer right away, Victoria added, "It's the lawyer, isn't it?"

"Vicky, why do I always fall for the wrong guy?"

"I don't know. If it helps, it doesn't get any easier when you find the right guy," Victoria said.

"What do you mean? Is there trouble in paradise with Mr. Mark Perfect?"

"You don't have to sound smug about it. Not really trouble. But he's still worried about his mom. He needs his trust fund."

"Just marry him," Tonya said. What was the big deal? It should be simple enough if they loved each other.

"I don't want him to propose just to get the trust fund," Victoria said.

"You know he cares about you or he wouldn't have ditched me," Tonya said.

"He does. But people don't get hitched the moment they fall in love with each other. It takes time. Unless you're Brandon."

"Right, Brandon. He eloped with Sylvia, right?"

"Yes, Sylvia, my client. It was the fastest courtship I've ever seen," Victoria said.

The doorbell rang.

"Good for him, I guess. Let me call you back. Vicky. There's someone at the door," Tonya said.

She hung up and opened the door.

When she was suddenly face to face with Patrick, she almost dropped her phone.

"What are you doing here?" she asked.

"You left this at the office, and I thought you might want it." He handed her the envelope with the scholarship folder.

She looked at him suspiciously. "You're supposed to sign it and mail it back. They sent it to you, because you're my employer."

He glanced at his shoes, seemingly at a loss for words.

"What are you really doing here?" she asked.

His blue eyes focused on her face. There was a hint of vulnerability she hadn't seen in him before. "I wanted to see you."

Tonya almost pinched herself to check if she was dreaming. He was here to see her. She wanted nothing more than to fall into his arms, but she needed to keep her wits about her. She couldn't let him treat her like this.

"You've seen me. Are you happy now?" She moved to close the door.

He held out his arm to stop her and spoke hurriedly. "Let me take you to lunch to celebrate your scholarship. And we can talk about everything then."

"Everything?" She looked at him skeptically.

He caught her expression and added carefully, "I meant you can tell me about your scholarship meeting."

"I don't know if it's a good idea," she said.

"I think it's a great idea because it's lunchtime." Patrick grinned, as if his confidence had returned. He excelled at making logical arguments.

As if on cue, her stomach growled. He was right about lunchtime, and she was hungry. Besides, who was she kidding? She would follow this man anywhere.

She ignored the voice in her head telling her she was making a huge mistake as she grabbed her purse and locked the door behind her. She followed him down the stairs.

"Let's take my car," Patrick said with an assured voice she didn't want to challenge. He opened the passenger door for her, and she got in.

When he got behind the steering wheel, she tensed up. She could smell his aftershave, and if she adjusted her hand, she could touch his arm.

Not that she was going to.

She started talking to keep her mind off those inappropriate thoughts. "My meeting went well. I think I impressed them with my presentation."

"Good. I'm glad to hear that." Patrick squared his jaw and nodded. "You deserve it. You're tenacious. You never give up. You can worm your way into anything."

"Like this job?"

He laughed, and she smiled at his good humor.

Suddenly, he asked, "Do you like Italian?"

"Yes. Who doesn't?"

"I know just the place then."

She expected him to take her to one of the many small local restaurants. But when he pulled up in front of Valentino's, her mouth gaped open.

Valentino's, an upscale Italian Restaurant in the middle of downtown Neuenhagen, catered to the upper class, much like the first-class seats on the airplane. Valet parking only, servers in tuxedos, and reservations impossible to get for the average citizen.

Tonya looked around in amazement as she walked in. This was probably the classiest place she had ever set foot in, even nicer than the fancy restaurant chosen for her engagement party. Tonya cringed as she thought about her current attire. Jeans and a long-sleeve shirt didn't quite fit with an upscale place.

"I didn't realize we would come here or I would have changed," she said.

"You look great," Patrick whispered as they followed the server to their table.

She blushed.

After they had ordered their meal, Patrick raised his glass to Tonya's. "To you. For all your help. I don't know what I would do without you."

She tasted the wine. It was exquisite and deserved its favored spot on the restaurant's wine list.

The waiter deftly deposited their plates between them, and Tonya inhaled the scent of freshly prepared pasta. It tasted even better than it looked. Tonya savored every bite but couldn't finish the lasagna she had ordered.

When she looked up, Patrick had cleared his plate and was taking another sip of wine. He had made his wineglass last through the entire meal.

She was already on her third or fourth glass. She couldn't remember, really. It was delicious, and she suddenly felt calmer and happier than she had in days. And why shouldn't she? She was having dinner at a restaurant with a man she liked.

As in, she liked him so much she wanted him for dinner and dessert.

Good thing he couldn't read her mind.

He asked, "How was your food?"

"It was great. I'm stuffed now."

"Would you like dessert?"

Was it her imagination, or did his question have an undertone? She closed her eyes for a second. There was no way he was flirting with her. He had already made it clear nothing else could happen between them. He just meant dessert.

"I think I want to go home," she said.

He was silent during the drive, and she didn't want to ask what he was thinking. He seemed tense, judging by the way his hands gripped the steering wheel.

When he pulled up to her apartment complex, she let out a big breath. He killed the engine and turned toward her. She wasn't sure what to say. 'Thanks for dinner' seemed too casual.

"See you tomorrow?" Tonya said as she grabbed her purse.

He nodded. Then he unbuckled and got up to open the car door for her. So much for keeping a distance of two feet.

"Thanks," she said as he slammed the passenger door shut behind her.

He took a step toward her and touched a loose strand of her hair with his hand. "I like it better when you wear your hair down."

Tonya's heart hammered in her chest. It almost seemed loud enough for him to hear. She could smell his scent, and his face was now inches from hers. He slowly bent down and closed the distance between them until she felt his lips on hers, soft and a little hesitant. He tasted like wine, deliciously sweet.

She wondered why he was kissing her, but the words wouldn't come out of her mouth. Her body just reacted to him. She kissed him back, gently at first. When his tongue explored her mouth, she moaned. Her hands grabbed the fabric of his shirt, and she could feel his firm chest underneath. His hands moved from her face down her back, pulling her closer to him. He started kissing her neck, and she dropped her purse.

Almost involuntarily, she took a step back. He looked at her, panting a little.

She needed to clear her head. "I don't understand what you're doing. What do you want?"

"I want you, Tonya."

Her heart was fluttering happily and her body was aching for him to touch her, but her logical side demanded an explanation.

"You were the one who gave me the cold shoulder."

"I was an idiot. But come on, you're my employee. Even you don't think this is a good idea, do you?" He took a step toward her.

"That's not really the reason, is it?" Tonya forced herself to keep talking. "I saw the video."

Patrick exhaled. "It feels like ancient history now."

"Didn't you get your heart broken in public?" Tonya asked.

"I did. At least, I thought I did," he said. "But knowing how I feel about you, I don't think I was in love with her."

Was she hearing things? Did Patrick have feelings for her?

"You're just saying that," Tonya whispered.

"I didn't want to like you. I didn't even want to hire you," he admitted.

She looked at him with distrust.

"When I first saw you standing at my door, I only saw her. And my first instinct was to shut the door in your face."

"You almost did."

He laughed deeply. "Have you ever been publicly humiliated by a guy like that?"

"Sort of. My fiancé broke up with me on the day of my wedding."

Now he was the one to wear a shocked expression on his face.

"It's not really a big deal," Tonya said. "I mean it was, but it's fine now. I'm fine."

She almost told him she hadn't loved the man, but the words didn't want to leave her mouth. He would think she was a gold digger.

And then he moved. He was too close to her again. She couldn't think straight.

He touched his forehead to hers and gently rubbed her arms. "This is probably a bad idea."

"Probably," she agreed as her breath was coming in faster.

If she was smart, she would get away from him and maybe look for another job. His lips found hers again, and Tonya moaned and put her arms around him.

So much for doing the smart thing.

His hands gently closed around her wrists just as he pulled away from the kiss. She opened her eyes in surprise. Why did he stop kissing her?

He said in a low growl, "What about Daron?"

"He's just a friend. There's nothing going on between us," Tonya said breathlessly.

It seemed to satisfy him, and his mouth was on hers again. Maybe it was the wine, maybe it was her long-standing crush on him, but she suddenly realized this was inevitable.

Tonya resolutely grabbed his hand and pulled him toward the house. He remembered to lock his car with his remote as they rushed up the stairs to her apartment.

Before she could unlock the door, he grabbed her and kissed her again. This time, there was no hesitation from either of them. Two feet away from her door, they were making out like lovesick teenagers. As he kissed her, his hand wandered under her shirt, making her skin tingle with anticipation.

"Just let me open the door," Tonya mumbled under her breath.

Patrick briefly let go while she dug for her keys. As she turned the keys in the lock, he started kissing her neck, wrapping his arms around her waist from behind.

They stumbled into the apartment, throwing off their shoes on the way to the bedroom. Patrick slammed the door shut with his foot. He took the purse out of her hand and dropped it in the hallway. They made it into her bedroom, where he gently pushed her onto the bed. His mouth was on hers again before he took off her shirt.

"You're beautiful, you know that?" His hands held her chin as he kissed her slowly. "I just can't get you out of my head."

Patrick shrugged out of his jacket, and Tonya pulled him on top of her by his tie. She kissed him on the lips, then loosened his tie and pulled it over his head. She unbuttoned his shirt while he took off her bra.

Patrick's shirt landed in a heap next to the bed. Her fingers touched his muscular chest and arms and trailed his abs.

Patrick lowered Tonya back down onto the bed and removed his pants. Her jeans followed in one swoop. A shiver of anticipation ran through her as she felt his almost naked body on hers. Her body was aching for him, but Patrick took his time with her.

He bent his head down and sucked on one nipple while rubbing the other with his finger before switching. He came up to kiss her on the mouth and suck on her neck while his hands wandered inside her panties.

She writhed against his fingers, which moved rhythmically inside her. He made quick work of her underwear and his, flinging them to the side without paying attention to where they landed.

His hand never lost his stride as he bent down and slowly kissed her lips, her chin, and her neck. She pulled him on top of her and wrapped her arms around his neck, willing him to come inside her.

Her fingers guided him and for one moment, neither of them moved as he filled her.

"You feel so good," Patrick whispered in her ear.

Tonya moaned. "So do you."

She wrapped her legs around him as they moved in unison, as tightly connected as possible. He started slowly, teasing her until she begged for more. He smiled and switched to long, hard strokes.

She reached blissful heights just before he did. They lay there silently for a while as millions of thoughts competed in her head.

She had slept with her boss. Again.

But it was more than just sex. She knew without a doubt she was in love with him. It would be easy to blame the wine she had with dinner, but she knew it wasn't the reason they had ended up in bed together.

Patrick lifted his head and kissed her gently on the lips. She shivered, suddenly feeling more tired than anything but not wanting to waste a moment with him in her bed.

Patrick retrieved her comforter from the floor and put it on the bed. He got in beside her and took her in his arms. She rested her head on his chest and took a deep breath. He kissed the top of her head, and she drifted off to sleep with a smile on her face.

Chapter 10

DURING THE NIGHT, Tonya got up and went to the bathroom. When she looked in the mirror, she noticed she hadn't even removed her makeup. She thought about the man in her bed as she brushed out her hair. What was going to happen to them now they had crossed that barrier again?

The last time, they could both pretend it was a vacation fling and meant nothing. What about this time?

When she tiptoed into the bedroom, she hesitated.

Then she heard his gravelly voice from the depths of the room. "Come back to bed, Tonya. It's cold without a blanket."

She loved hearing him call her by her first name. It was oddly sexual after the distance he had created between them. And he was right. It was cold. When she climbed in, his arms reached out to her and pulled her in beside him.

"Let me warm you up, gorgeous."

They had already done the deed. There was no harm in doing it again. They could always talk later.

His thoughts seemed to run along the same lines. His hands slowly stroked her back and thighs and his mouth kissed hers softly, without hurry. He seemed determined to take advantage of the rest of the night, exploring her body with his mouth. She moaned and wrapped her arms around him. She grabbed his firm buttocks and walked her fingers up and down his strong back. She could feel his erection pressing against her.

This time, she would take charge. She rolled on top of him and positioned herself upright. When their bodies joined, she deliberately held still, until he grabbed her hips and moaned. She started moving slowly as his fingers explored her body. When his thumb rubbed against her clitoris, she moaned. She found her rhythm. When she finally came again, he reached the peak with her.

They slept in each other's arms until sunlight streamed through the windows. When she woke up, she found him watching her. His blue eyes had a satisfied glow about them.

He was still here. She wanted to pinch herself. She had feared he would disappear like last time.

"Good morning, gorgeous," he said as he kissed her cheek.

"What time is it?"

"Oh, shit."

He sat up, and the comforter fell off him, revealing his muscular chest and arms. He was the beautiful one, Tonya thought, as she watched him look for a clock in her room. He finally pulled his cell phone out of his pants pocket and relaxed a little.

"It's only eight. We'll be fine."

"I need to take a shower and get dressed. I'll see you at the office?"

"Okay."

She kissed him briefly on the lips.

"Maybe we shouldn't go to work," he said, pulling her to him, his mouth on hers again.

Tonya laughed and shook her head, twisting out of his embrace.

When she showed up at work an hour later, Patrick was waiting for her with a cup of latte macchiato. She was the luckiest woman in the world. Here was this incredibly hot lawyer making her favorite drink.

The *Perfect* Plan

"We need to talk," Patrick said as Tonya put her purse on her desk.

She looked up in alarm. They had just slept together. What could be wrong now?

"Before you freak out, it's not that bad."

"Just tell me." Tonya stood up, an uneasy feeling coming over her. Something bad was going to happen. She just knew it.

"I've wanted you when I first laid eyes on you, but you're still my employee. What we're doing here isn't really a good idea." He scratched his head. "I don't really know how to say this."

"Just get to the point."

"I need you to quit," he said abruptly.

"What?"

Quit? He wanted her to quit her job? She shook her head in confusion and walked behind the safety of her desk, trying to make sense of what he was saying.

"Look, you're smart and talented. You'll find another job. I'll write you a glowing recommendation."

"I don't understand. I've been working my ass off for you."

"Tonya, don't you get it?" He got up and walked toward her, taking her hands in his across the desk. "I want to be with you. I want you to be my girlfriend. I want to take you upstairs and do all sorts of unspeakable things to you."

Her face flushed, remembering last night's encounter with him. She certainly felt the same.

"But you can't be my employee. You can't work for me."

"But... I don't understand."

"I know it's a big deal." His eyes pleaded with her. "But I just can't be involved with my employee. I'll find a guy to replace you. It was the original plan, anyway."

"This has been a great job for me. I've been able to do real paralegal work for the first time."

Tonya swallowed hard. This was a tremendous disappointment for her. She would have to give up this job and miss helping people like the Sheffields. If she didn't get the scholarship, she might have to work as a secretary again.

Then another thought occurred to her. She wouldn't get the recommendation if she didn't work here.

"What about my scholarship? I need to be employed to qualify."

"I already gave you the employment reference. If it doesn't pan out, I'll pay for your school. It's no big deal," he said. "Please? Do it for me."

His hands were now pulling her to him, even though the desk between them forbade a close embrace. He leaned into her and kissed her slowly on the lips.

She moaned. "I'll quit right now."

He smiled and continued kissing her. "We could go to my office and see what's under your skirt." His lips were now exploring her cleavage.

"You have appointments, Patrick." She pushed him away.

He shrugged. "It would be difficult to get any work done around here with you."

She grinned. He was just flattering her, but it was balm for her soul.

"Just work in your office," she said.

"What do you think I've been doing these past weeks to stop myself from touching you?"

"Really?"

He nodded. Then he blew her a kiss and turned on his heels to go to his office.

Tonya sat at her desk for a moment, contemplating what he said. He cared about her, and he wanted to be with her. She only had to make one small sacrifice. Quit her job. But she would go to law school soon, and the scholarship was practically hers. Patrick didn't need to pay for her tuition. He had already given her an employment reference, which was all she needed.

Still, it bothered her.

She picked up the phone and called the women's shelter to update Sabrina on her case.

"Hi Sabrina, I just wanted to let you know we filed the paperwork. Now we just have to wait."

"Great, thank you. Will I have to appear in court?"

"No, probably not. Your ex doesn't have a lawyer and is not contesting the charges. You'll have to go in six months from now when the divorce is final, but we can cross that bridge when we get to it. Given the situation, I'm certain we can get you in and out without him knowing about it."

"Thank you, Tonya. I appreciate your help." Sabrina said.

"It was the least I could do," Tonya said.

She was as relieved as Sabrina it had gone down smoothly. The people at the shelter would help her get a fresh start and move her and her child to a different city or even out of state, and she would only have to come back to finalize the divorce. It was a clean slate for Sabrina. She deserved it.

Patrick came out of the office, talking animatedly into his phone. He waved at her as he jogged up the stairs to his apartment.

Tonya had never even been upstairs. But soon...

It was time to decide. Which would it be? Her job or Patrick?

She really had no choice, did she?

Before she could second guess her decision, Tonya cleaned up her desk. She stacked the important paperwork in one pile, with notes attached to each folder and carried it into Patrick's office. Someone else would have to deal with it. It made her sad. She didn't want to find another job.

When she deposited the paperwork on his desk, she noticed a paper on the floor. Maybe she had accidentally pushed it off.

She picked it up and was about to add it to the others when the words on it caught her attention. It was an employment contract. What was her employment contract doing here?

She began reading it from the top and realized with a start it was a contract between Patrick Rhodes and Vince Coleman. Weird. Had he already replaced her? She looked at the date and her eyes widened in shock.

Vince had been working for Patrick for three weeks.

Vince was the guy who had been here weeks ago. She couldn't find a record of his appointment, but Patrick saw him right away. Why hadn't she asked about it then? It was clearly out of character for Patrick to see someone without an appointment.

She hadn't even questioned Vince's presence, although she had wondered at the lack of paperwork then. But she had been busy working on the other cases, especially the Sheffield file. In the meantime, Patrick had interviewed Vince and hired him. To replace her.

She looked at the date again. Patrick had replaced her before anything had ever happened between them. Was this all just a ruse?

She stood up, blood rushing to her face. He had kissed her and slept with her just to get rid of her. And now he was telling her to quit because he didn't want to date his employee.

He had been lying to her the entire time. And she believed he cared about her.

She heard footsteps on the stairs.

How stupid she had been.

When he walked into the office, he stared at the phone in his hand in confusion.

"Tonya, there's something I need to ask..." When he saw her expression, he frowned. "What's wrong?"

Tonya crossed her arms in front of her chest and took a deep breath.

"You hired Vince Coleman to replace me, didn't you?"

"What?"

"You've been trying to figure out how to get rid of me for weeks. You already have a replacement," she said.

"What are you talking about?"

"I know you didn't want to hire me. You said it yourself. Then I blackmailed you into it. Then you had this brilliant idea to get me to quit. You just had to pretend you liked me." She could hear herself getting louder. She would not let him see how much he had hurt her.

"I'm not pretending anything," Patrick said.

"You didn't interview Vince three weeks ago?"

"Well yes, but..."

"Why would you interview another person when you already have an employee for the job? You were trying to get rid of me." Tonya's voice shook a little. "Well, you'll have to fire me if you want to hire someone else. I'm not quitting."

"Let's back up for a second here." Patrick's brow furrowed.

"You've wanted to fire me all along," Tonya whispered.

"No. I mean, yes. But not for the reasons you think," Patrick said. "Tonya, I didn't want to get involved with you or anyone. I thought it would be easier to just hire Vince and let you go. I didn't think I was going to fall in..."

"Don't say it," Tonya interrupted him. "You should have told me about Vince."

"It's not like you always tell the truth," Patrick said.

"What are you talking about?"

"Why would you agree to marry a guy for money?" Patrick asked.

Tonya looked at him in confusion. "What are you talking about?"

"Two can play this game. You said your last boyfriend left you at the altar, but you failed to mention you only wanted to marry him for money."

Tonya could feel the blood rushing to her cheeks. He had been digging around in her past without her knowledge.

"That has nothing to do with us. You hiring someone else does."

"It doesn't? You don't look for wealthy guys to marry? You didn't want to marry Mark or maybe Daron?"

"I didn't end up marrying anyone," Tonya said.

"But you would have."

She couldn't deny it. She avoided his eyes and heard him curse under his breath.

"I was on the phone with Vince just now."

"Patrick, this is just a big misunderstanding."

"You weren't originally looking for a husband to pay for your law school?"

He closed the gap between them and tilted her chin up. His blue eyes scrutinized hers. She knew the truth was written there.

She had been looking for a husband to pay for school. It was the reason she wanted to marry Mark. A hot denial was on her lips, but she closed her mouth again.

"I see." He nodded and put his hands in his pocket.

"I don't expect anything from you," she said truthfully. "That was then. I wanted to marry someone to get into law school, but it didn't happen. I got a job here instead. And I applied for scholarships. You and I have nothing to do with what happened then."

She blinked away tears. She was in love with him. Couldn't he see that?

"I can't believe this," Patrick said. "Why haven't you ever told me?"

Suddenly, she was angry. "You hired someone behind my back. You're the one to talk. You've been pretending to like me this entire time and spying on me behind my back."

He had played her for a fool.

"Tonya, I hired this guy before the stuff between us happened. I wanted to fire you. But now things are different. I can't have a relationship with my employee. We agreed on this. We can't work in the same office and still be together."

She shook her head. She had been blind and stupid. She had believed he genuinely cared for her. But she was wrong again.

"It won't be a problem, Mr. Rhodes." Tonya glared at him. "I have no problem honoring the two-foot rule as agreed per our employment contract."

"What are you doing?" His arms reached out to her, but she skirted around him and left his office.

"I'm not quitting. You can tell that Vince guy to go back to where he came from."

"Tonya..."

"Please call me Miss Corley, Mr. Rhodes." Tonya sat down on her chair and turned toward her computer screen.

"You're kidding me, right?"

"Is there anything you'd like me to work on, Mr. Rhodes? Your next client is coming in ten minutes."

She turned her face away from him, even though it cost her more self-control than she thought she had. She would not break down and cry about it. She could be professional, and she would show him he couldn't mess with her.

She felt him approach her chair from behind and knew he was going to touch her, maybe even try to kiss her. She had to stop him, or she wouldn't be able to keep up the wall between them.

"Don't touch me, Mr. Rhodes. You can't afford a harassment lawsuit."

Her tone was icy and seemed to hit just the right note. She could hear him take in a big breath.

"I shouldn't have hired someone to dig into your background. But you should have told me the truth, too. How could I believe you're not just in it for the money?" He took a deep breath. "I care about you, Tonya."

She swiveled around in her chair to face him.

"Don't lie to me. You interviewed this man while I was working here. You meant to replace me this entire time. All the while, I've been working my butt off for you." Tonya gritted her teeth and was about to release another stream of venom when the door opened. She lowered her voice and said, "I'm not quitting. You'll just have to fire me if you want to get rid of me. Now excuse me, Mr. Rhodes, I have work to do."

She faced the woman who had just walked in and smiled. "Hello, what can I do for you?"

Tonya could feel him shoot a pleading glance at her, but she didn't look in his direction.

***

Five minutes after Tonya got home, her mother stood in front of her door. So much for getting drunk and forgetting the events of the day. Tonya forced herself to smile in welcome, but her mother wasn't even paying attention.

"I brought you some muffins, and I got your mail for you." Darlene Corley sat on the couch, a plate of untouched muffins in front of her.

Tonya grabbed a muffin and ate it in two bites. When her hand reached out for another muffin, she met her mother's astonished glance. Tonya shrugged and took a bite of the second muffin. She had nothing to lose at this point. A few carbohydrates couldn't make the situation any worse.

"Your father talked to Aunt Allyson," Darlene said.

"Really? How did it happen? And what did she say?"

"He said he had finally had enough of me yapping on about my sister," Darlene said, clearly hurt by her husband's words but also immensely pleased with his interference. "He took matters into his own hands and tracked her down. They had a great talk. I don't know if he got through to her, but she knows we're here to help."

"Wow. That's wonderful news," Tonya said.

She smiled, picturing her father arm in arm with Aunt Allyson. Maybe there was hope for her.

Tonya was about to grab another muffin when she remembered the mail. She sifted through the letters and dropped three of them unopened in the garbage.

"What if it's something important?" Darlene asked.

"It's just junk..." Tonya's hands stopped in midair.

The last letter wasn't junk. It was from the scholarship Daron had told her about. She hastily tore open the envelope and her eyes flew over the page.

Dear Miss Corley,
We regret to inform you

She dropped the letter on the floor. Tonya felt like someone had punched her in the gut. She didn't qualify for the scholarship. It had all seemed too good to be true.

Now there was no light at the end of the tunnel where her job was concerned. How many years would she have to work to save up enough for college?

Tonya let out an anguished sigh. "I can't believe this."

"What's wrong?" Tonya's mother looked up.

"My scholarship. It got denied. It says I missed a deadline to turn in... but I thought I sent it. It must have been during the Savannah trip. I mailed it as soon as we got back."

"A few days surely won't matter," Darlene said.

"Yes, they do, Mom."

"You can still go to law school," Darlene said.

Tonya shook her head desolately. This was her best shot at law school, and she blew it. She might as well quit her job, too. Maybe she needed to pursue another career altogether.

Chapter 11

WHEN TONYA WALKED into the office the next day, she still didn't know what to do. To protect herself from heartache, she really needed to quit. But she also had to pay the bills, even if law school was out of reach.

Then the letter from Parachute Executives arrived. She had been waiting to hear from them since her last formal reply. In the past, they had called her right after receiving her mail and set up a meeting to talk about settling the case. They seemed less eager now, and she worried they had turned down their settlement offer too many times. Or maybe they had reached the maximum amount of what they would offer?

The letter invited Mr. Rhodes to come to their office again and finalize the settlement or otherwise proceed with the lawsuit. From the research Tonya had done, she knew it wasn't out of the ordinary to word it this way. It was time to wrap up the case for both parties, and there was nothing like the threat of a long, drawn-out lawsuit to increase the pressure.

Tonya got up and knocked on the door of Patrick's, no Mr. Rhodes', office. She kept her distance, even though he had tried several times to talk to her. He hadn't come close enough to touch her, thanks to his own stupid two-foot rule. Tonya wasn't sure how she felt about this.

She missed him.

"Come in."

Tonya opened the door and peeked in. He was sitting at his desk, tie slightly askew. When he saw her, he smiled. When she didn't return his smile, his facial expression became resigned.

"What can I do for you?"

He refused to call her Miss Corley, even though she continued to use his last name. He avoided using her name altogether.

"Parachute Executives wrote a letter. They want to have another meeting, and they want it to be the final one." Tonya waved the letter in her hand.

"Excellent. Let's do it."

"I think we should talk to the Sheffields. I can go to their house after work to save them the trip over here. We need to know for which amount they would settle."

"That's probably better than doing it over the phone."

Tonya asked, "What do you think their max is?"

They both knew she was speaking about Parachute now, not the Sheffields. They had speculated over how much they could recover for the Sheffields, but it hinged on a lot of different things.

"Ideally, they'll pay for lawyer fees and return all the money the Sheffields have lost. We may have to contend with much less."

"Having a sizeable chunk of the money back would be better for the Sheffields than a lawsuit worth three times the amount."

He agreed, "Very true. Please talk to the clients. Tell them we can't decide for them, but we'll call from Parachute's offices in Savannah to present the next offer to them. They can decide then. Let me know what time the meeting is, and I'll make the arrangements for our flight."

Tonya nodded. "Sounds good." Then she added, "Did you want to read this?"

"Absolutely."

Tonya stepped into the office and deposited the paper at the edge of his desk before backing away again.

"You're being ridiculous," Patrick said, commenting on her efforts to avoid him.

"One can't be too careful," she said. "It's in the contract, which you wrote."

He mumbled something incomprehensible as she closed the door behind her.

***

On her drive to the Sheffields' house, Tonya turned up the volume on the radio to escape her thoughts and feelings. If it hurt this much to just be around him every day, it was time to quit her job and soon. Her feelings for him wouldn't fade just because he had turned out to be a manipulating liar.

She needed to make sure he wrote her a glowing recommendation to help with her job search. It was the least he could do for her.

As she pulled up in front of the Sheffields' house, it dismayed her to see the grass was higher than it had been last time. They probably didn't have anyone to mow it for them. She was momentarily filled with hatred for Parachute Executives for dragging the settlement talks out when they could just make it right. She swallowed her anger and knocked on the door.

Mrs. Sheffield greeted her at the door. "Thank you for coming, my dear. Come on in. Can I offer you some coffee or a cookie?"

"No, thank you. I appreciate you meeting with me on such short notice."

"We have little else going on, Miss Corley."

Tonya followed Mrs. Sheffield to the living room and took a seat on the low couch.

"Where is Mr. Sheffield?"

"He's taking a nap. This stuff is wearing him out, I'm afraid."

Tonya pulled out the letter she had received. "I don't have any news just yet, but we have another meeting with Parachute Executives in Savannah the day after tomorrow. They sent a letter asking us to fly out there again. From their wording, it sounds like they want to come to an agreement and put this case behind them."

Mrs. Sheffield nodded. "Are they ready to give us back our money?"

"It doesn't say. They won't make us their offer until we get there. And it may be their last offer."

"Do we have to take whatever they offer us?"

"No. You're not obligated to accept an offer from them. You still have the option to go through the court system."

"Dear, we've talked about this," Mrs. Sheffield said reprovingly. "Mr. Sheffield and I don't have the luxury of time on our side."

Tonya felt crestfallen. "Right. Yes, I guess you're right then. We're doing the best we can."

"I know, dear. I know. Mr. Rhodes is a highly qualified lawyer and a decent human being." Mrs. Sheffield leaned back in her chair and shot Tonya an innocent smile. "He's a rather nice-looking young man, too, isn't he?"

Tonya smiled but wasn't sure what to say.

"I remember meeting Mr. Sheffield when I was only twenty years old. He thought he knew everything, and I really didn't like him." She chuckled. "He tried mighty hard to woo me."

Tonya listened with rapt attention. "How did you know you were meant to be together?"

"I couldn't be without him. It was as simple as that, honey."

What an outdated idea. Nowadays, a woman could easily be without a man. A woman didn't need a man at all.

"I can see by the look on your face you don't believe me. But when you find the right one, you just know. And nothing else will matter."

"We should probably talk to your husband about the case," Tonya said, trying to change the subject.

"For now, we'll let him sleep. But what do you want us to do? You want us to pick a big enough number, don't you?"

Tonya shrugged. "Yes, kind of."

"To be honest, we'll take whatever they'll give us at this point. It's been really difficult to make do, and none of us are fit to work like when we were younger."

"I understand."

"You'll know what to do, Miss Corley. And I know Mr. Rhodes will do the right thing."

Tonya caught Mrs. Sheffield watching her with an odd smile on her face. Did she know something was going on between her and Mr. Rhodes?

"Mr. Rhodes is my employer. He's not... I mean..."

Mrs. Sheffield chuckled. "He liked you well enough. But maybe I'm wrong. Maybe you have another sweetheart. I hope he's good enough for you."

Tonya tried to smile. If this woman only knew.

"Thank you. And you will talk to Mr. Sheffield about the case? I can come by again later maybe and explain it to him if you like."

"No, it's fine. Call us when you have another offer to present, and we'll hope for the best."

**

Tonya arrived early at the office. It would be a busy day, especially with their impromptu flight to Savannah the next day. She warily spent an hour rescheduling the appointments.

When the front door opened and Patrick strode in, Tonya looked up in confusion. Why was Patrick coming in through the front door this time of day? Where had he been?

"Good morning," he said, smiling.

Why did he look so chipper?

Suddenly, she wondered if he had spent the night with another woman. It would explain why he wasn't coming from upstairs. No wonder he was smiling. Tonya averted her eyes, but his step had a bounce to it when he walked into his office. The idea of him seeing someone else was more than she could handle.

She had to quit. She couldn't be around him anymore without being reminded of her heartbreak. What did she have to lose at this point? She had to quit now before she changed her mind.

"Mr. Rhodes?"

Patrick turned around slowly.

"I'm quitting. Consider this my two-week notice."

He walked up to her desk, and his eyes looked hopeful. "Are you quitting because I asked you to?"

"No. I'm just quitting. Vince will be ecstatic," she said, her voice dripping with sarcasm.

"Tonya..."

"It's Miss Corley."

He waved his hand in irritation. "Please don't leave like this. I already mailed your employment reference to the scholarship people. And last week, I got a request to verify your earnings. What if you don't get the scholarship? You'll need a job to qualify for student loans."

He sounded genuinely concerned. And yet, she felt bitter. It wasn't any of his business what she did to get into law school.

"I'm not getting the scholarship. I got a letter a couple of days ago. Anyway, I can't stay here like this." Tonya almost stumbled over her words, because Patrick was looking at her again with those earnest blue eyes. "I'll help you wrap things up. I want to take care of the Sheffields."

He nodded slowly. "If that's what you want."

"Yes. I think it's better this way," Tonya said with a lump in her throat.

He had protested a little, but on some level, he must feel relieved she was finally leaving. He had wanted this all along.

"Alright." He shut the door to his office, and she felt utterly alone.

She was making the right decision, she told herself. She could survive two more weeks with him, even another trip to Savannah.

Chapter 12

THIS TIME, TONYA WAS BETTER prepared for the flight. She wore headphones and ignored Patrick the entire trip. And she kept thinking about the two nights they had spent together and how hopeful she had felt when he originally asked her to resign. And now they were Miss Corley and Mr. Rhodes to each other.

Tonya took a deep breath. She could do this just a little longer.

When the plane landed, they hurried through the Atlanta airport again. It was almost like having a Déjà vu. Everything was the same, except it wasn't.

They sat next to each other on the small airplane. This time, there were no crying babies. Tonya pretended to be asleep. Patrick signed for the rental car again, and before she knew it, they had arrived at the building of Parachute Executives. This time, the place was bustling with activity.

As they crammed into the elevator with five other people, Tonya almost lost her balance when an elderly gentleman hit her with his briefcase on the way out. She felt Patrick's steadying arm on her.

"I got you," he said.

"Thanks."

He released her, and she leaned against the wall. She felt slightly shaken.

This was ridiculous. If she couldn't ride in an elevator with him without feeling her heart rate go through the roof, she couldn't work with him. It was a good thing she quit. All the money in the world wasn't worth this heartache. Surely, she would eventually get over him if she didn't have to see him every day.

Jack Hayes welcomed them to the conference room, and a secretary brought coffee and water for everyone.

When everyone had taken their seats, Jack Hayes stood up. Conversations ceased instantly around him. His team worked together like a well-run machine.

"Patrick and Tonya, it's nice to have you back here with us. While we enjoy your company, we hope this is the last time we'll see you about this case."

His comment elicited a few laughs around the table. Tonya noticed Patrick was smiling politely. It was hard to appreciate the humor in the situation. They weren't here to party. They were here to right a wrong.

Looking around the room, she didn't think anyone else felt that way. The other lawyers were just doing their job.

Jack continued, "We have come together as a team and put together a very generous offer. Now before you say anything about it, hear me out fully. This is not the only case we have to work on. There have been dozens of other cases much like this one. I believe you represent quite a few of those, too."

Tonya nodded along while Patrick remained motionless. They had been in touch with Jack Hayes about the other clients. Patrick would negotiate each case one at a time, and his strategy made sense to Tonya. It didn't concern her that the other lawyers had even more cases than they did. Cobblestone Investments had deep pockets.

Jack looked at his notes. "We have to settle every case for a reasonable amount to make sure everyone gets their money back, or at least a good portion of it. Now you know a sizeable chunk is going to the individual lawyers representing these clients, including yourself. That's money Cobblestone Investments didn't generate. It's coming out of our pockets. The big boss is not too happy, as you can imagine."

Patrick nodded along. Tonya glanced at him. Jack Hayes was telling them nothing new. They had been over the numbers a million times.

He slid the paper across the table with a number written on it.

$600,000.

"We're returning an extra twenty percent to the Sheffields. That's $100,000 more than they gave Cobblestone Investments. A good return on investment, I think." Jack Hayes smirked.

Tonya's shoulders fell as she did the math in her head. At twenty-five percent commission, the Sheffields would get $450,000. She felt a nudge on her shoulder and looked over at Patrick. She raised her eyebrows questioningly.

They were at a crossroads now. She was certain Parachute had reached their ceiling, and by the look on his face, she was sure Patrick agreed.

"Thank you for your offer, Jack," Patrick said. "Can you give us a few minutes to discuss this and call our clients?"

"Absolutely. There's a room next door you're welcome to use."

"Thank you, Jack." Patrick got up and grabbed his briefcase.

Tonya followed him to the room on the right. She hadn't even noticed it last time. She realized soon enough why. The room was smaller than her bathroom, with a desk crammed in one corner and two chairs beside it.

Patrick closed the door behind them and Tonya took a seat while he remained standing.

"This offer gives them $450,000. I'm sure they'll take it," Tonya said.

"It doesn't feel right to take such a large cut. I want them to get their money back. $100,000 is a great fee for this case. We've settled it in record time. And their neighbors will be in the same boat."

"The neighbors will want the same percentage," Tonya pointed out.

Patrick waved her concerns away. "They won't know the percentages. They get the same contract. If we end up in the same situation, I can evaluate on a case-by-case basis. I still have to keep the lights on and pay your salary."

There was an awkward pause between them. He wouldn't be paying her salary for much longer.

Tonya asked, "Shall I call the Sheffields and present his offer?"

"Yes, please do."

"Am I telling them about your offer to reduce your commission?"

"Yes," he said.

"It should be you calling them." He was making the sacrifice. He should get the credit for it.

He shook his head. "You're better at explaining things without using legalese. And you're getting a bonus to do the work, aren't you?"

Tonya nodded slowly. She was getting a percentage of the profits.

"Don't worry. Just because I'm taking less of a cut doesn't change yours."

She shot him an annoyed look. "Is that what you think of me? I'm only worried about money?"

"Well, no."

"Yes, you do." She exhaled in exasperation. "Whatever. It doesn't matter." She got up and pushed past him, almost stumbling to get to the door. "Excuse me. I'm going to call the Sheffields now."

He grabbed her hand, trying to stop her from leaving. "Tonya, please let's talk about this."

She turned around and looked up at him. "Do you really think I wanted to be with you for your money? And to get a ring on my finger?"

She saw doubt flicker across his face before he answered, "No."

She withdrew her hand from his.

"Don't be ridiculous. Tonya..."

"Just don't."

She couldn't focus this close to him. He was inches away from her, and she wanted him to kiss her and hold her and make everything better.

It would be temporary.

Her hand found the doorknob, and she let herself out of the room. It took her a minute to catch her breath.

The phone call to the Sheffields took a while. Tonya explained the arrangement carefully. Twice. Then she heard the two of them whooping and hollering. It made her laugh.

Mrs. Sheffield thanked her profusely for working hard on their behalf. "Mr. Rhodes is a mighty nice man to do this for us. I knew he had it in him when I first met him. You don't meet too many men who'll open car doors for you anymore."

Tonya smiled, but her heart wasn't in it. Patrick was a nice guy. She couldn't deny it. As she hung up, she heard a door close quietly behind her. Patrick had come into the hallway, careful to keep his distance. He looked at her questioningly.

"They're ecstatic." Tonya pointed to the phone.

He smiled, but the smile didn't reach his eyes. "I'm glad. They deserve it."

It took another thirty minutes to sign the paperwork. The mood in the room was jovial. The secretary brought muffins and pastries, which the lawyers devoured hastily. This was just the beginning of the day for them. They would negotiate with other people for several more hours.

She was going to miss this, she decided.

Just because she was quitting this job didn't mean she couldn't work somewhere else and do more of the same thing. She could always move and find a job as a paralegal in another city.

***

With the case was closed, there was nothing left to do. Tonya had insisted on staying in a hotel room this time. There was just no way she could stay under the same roof with Patrick. He had said little when she told him this earlier. He had merely nodded.

Back on the sidewalk in front of Parachute Executives, she looked at the reservation on her phone. It wasn't time to check in yet, but it would take a while to get there. As she pulled up the map, Patrick spoke.

"Would you like a ride?"

"I was just going to walk," she said.

He looked stern. "You want to walk through all of downtown? Is your hotel even within walking distance?"

She showed him the map on her phone.

He shook his head immediately. "You're not walking. Just get in the car."

His offer seemed innocent enough. And he was right. The hotel wasn't exactly around the corner. She shrugged and wordlessly got into the passenger seat.

It was unnerving to sit next to him like this again. This time, she couldn't wear headphones and ignore him. Whenever she looked at him, her heart ached. Her gaze drifted to the window instead.

She would never appreciate Savannah's beauty because the city was forever linked with Patrick. Love ruined things.

It always had for her.

Patrick expertly swung into a parking spot on a side street. He turned off the engine and turned toward her. Tonya looked around in confusion. There was no hotel in sight. Were they even in the right part of town? She hadn't paid attention to the street names as they had passed them. Not that it would have helped her. She didn't know the city.

"Where are we?"

"Let's go for a walk. It's too early for you to check in," Patrick said.

Tonya sighed. She had been planning to wait in the hotel lobby. Away from him. Then she looked out of the window again. Something about her surroundings suddenly seemed familiar to her. Before she had decided, Patrick opened her door and held out his hand. She stepped out of the car without taking his hand. He seemed frustrated and stuck his hands in his pockets as she slowly walked alongside him.

"Where are we going?"

"Give it a moment. You'll see," he said with a smile on his lips.

"I'm still quitting."

"Tonya, I don't care whether you quit or not. I mean, I enjoy working with you, but it's kind of distracting, too."

"What?"

"Look, don't you see? I love you," he said.

She shook her head, not wanting to believe what he was saying to her. But he continued talking.

"I already told you why I didn't want to hire you at first. Then you hooked up the computers, and I was impressed, but I still didn't want to get involved with anyone, which is why I sent you away." He smiled at the memory. "But you came back to blackmail me."

"I'm sorry," Tonya said.

"I'm not." He paused a moment before he continued. "It was difficult to keep my hands off of you in the office. I thought about a way to have it all—I wanted to date you, but I didn't want you to work for me. I played with the idea of letting you go. I shouldn't have gone behind your back about it. I had Vince all lined up to take your place, but then I couldn't do it. He needed work right away and was going to find another job, so I hired him. When I ran out of projects for him, I asked him to do some detective work."

He paused and glanced at her before his gaze shifted to their surroundings.

She had been drawn into his narrative and hadn't even noticed where her feet were taking her. As they turned the corner, she recognized the enormous fountain. He had brought her back to Forsyth Park. A place she adored.

Then she looked at him. "Why did you dig into my background?"

"I got carried away. Vince needed something to do." Patrick sighed. "Then you walked into my room at Aunt Mildred's house. And everything changed."

"Except nothing changed," she said. He had put up a distance between them.

"I didn't want to get involved because of what happened in my last relationship. It was stupid." He reached for her hands and pulled her to the side of the path. "I just wasn't ready. It was bad timing, Tonya."

"I don't know what to say."

"Tell me this; do you even care about me?"

"I do," she said truthfully.

No point in lying now.

He took her face in his hands and gently brushed her hair to the side. His lips met hers, and she was transported into another world for a moment. Then he drew back a little, his hand under her chin.

"What about those other guys? Why were you trying to get married for money? That's not what this is, is it?"

"No," she said. "It's different with you."

"Tell me the truth about everything, Tonya."

"I wanted to get into law school. I got accepted to start this fall and Mark was going to pay for it. But then he fell in love with someone else." She remembered being left at the altar. Not her best day. "I didn't get married. I got a job instead. With you."

"Why did you agree to marry that Mark guy? And what about Daron? Were you going to marry him? Is it just about going to law school for you?" Patrick took a seat on the bench next to her. He wasn't touching her, but she could feel his hands by her side. "Why would you get married for a degree? Why not apply for student loans?"

She sighed. She might as well tell him now. He already knew the worst of it.

"My ex wrecked my credit."

"The cheater?"

"Yes, Nick, the cheater. I couldn't get a loan, not even student loans." Tonya spread her arms, remembering the desperation she had felt. "I wanted to go to law school to make a difference. My aunt was the victim of domestic violence. She had nobody to help her when she needed help most."

"That's tough."

Tonya nodded. "I assumed becoming a lawyer would make the biggest impact. It has been one of my dreams for a long time."

"You've been making a difference here, too," he whispered.

Tonya blinked, surprised. He was right, in a way. She had been making a difference. For the Sheffields. For Sabrina.

"Anyway. Mark was marrying me for money, too. He needed to get access to his trust fund." She caught his incredulous glance and explained, "It's not as bad as it seems. His mother has cancer, and he needed the money to pay for treatments."

"It makes it hard to hate the guy."

"You're telling me." Tonya laughed a little.

"I'm sorry." He kissed her again.

"I'm still quitting," she said, a little breathless.

"Fine with me. It might be easier to work on my cases if you're not in the next room, tempting me."

She pulled away from him. "You still shouldn't have gone behind my back and dug into my past."

"I'm sorry. Can you forgive me?"

Tonya shrugged. "It's not just that."

Patrick held her hand. "Look, I know you want to keep working here. I've been thinking about it, and I found a loophole."

"A loophole?"

"Yes. It's the perfect plan. You can work here with me, and we can be together."

"Okay..."

Where was he going with this?

"Marry me, Tonya."

"You're kidding me, right?" When she saw the hurt expression on his face, she added gently, "This is too soon."

He seemed genuinely confused. "If marriage isn't what you want, what is it?"

"I just want to be with you, silly."

Patrick pulled her in close and kissed her on the lips. "I love you, Tonya."

"I love you, too," she said.

He smiled.

"Oh, I almost forgot." He reached into his jacket pocket and pulled out a piece of paper. "There's something I wanted to show you."

He handed her a paper. Tonya started perusing it, but she couldn't concentrate. The word Athens caught her eye.

She looked at him. "What is this?"

"I met with a travel agent the other day," he said. "I booked a trip to Athens for Christmas. It will be a little chilly, but I think..." His voice trailed off as he grinned at her sheepishly.

"Are you kidding? You bought this for us?"

"I bought it for you. And of course, I'd love to go with you..."

"What about your clients? I thought they came first?"

"That's an outdated rule," he murmured as he started kissing her neck.

She moaned as he trailed kisses up her jaw line.

He murmured, "I say we ask for an early check-in."

They couldn't keep their hands off each other. They practically raced back to the car. When she got in beside him, he pulled her toward him and kissed her.

"Just drive," she said.

As he put the car into gear, his right hand grazed her thigh. She put her hand on his, and their fingers interlocked. The trees whizzed by, and a few minutes later they walked into the lobby of the hotel. Patrick held her hand as if he feared she would run away. She squeezed his hand reassuringly while he talked to the hotel staff.

The receptionist took an excruciating twenty minutes until she handed Patrick the room keys. He thanked her abruptly and pulled Tonya along with him.

"Should we get our stuff from the car?"

"Later," he said impatiently.

Before the doors of the elevator had completely closed, Patrick's lips were on hers and his hand wandered under her blouse.

She kissed him back greedily. The elevator dinged, and she pulled her blouse down. She didn't even know what room number they had, but Patrick was a man on a mission. He opened the door to the room with a flourish and locked it behind him.

The room turned out to be a suite. Tonya carefully sat down on the couch in the sitting area when Patrick strode in behind her.

Before she could say anything to him, he sat next to her and pulled her close. His hands and mouth were all over her. He impatiently unbuttoned her blouse while she fought with his tie.

She laughed a little at their hurry to get each other naked. "We have all the time in the world."

"No, we don't. We still have to work." He had flung her blouse and bra to the side and was now sliding her skirt down. His fingers found her wet and ready for him.

She moaned and whispered, "What about tonight?"

"Yeah. I'm going to need you to pull an all-nighter," he mumbled as he cupped her breasts.

Tonya moaned in response. She couldn't think of anything she would rather do.

She had unbuttoned his shirt, and he flung it off. Patrick sent the rest of their clothes flying and basked in the sight of her naked body. He was still sitting on the couch and guided her on top of him.

He groaned as she started slowly moving up and down. His hands traveled down her back and cupped her buttocks, gently squeezing her. She bent down to kiss him, and his tongue found her mouth. She gently bit his lower lip.

"Tonya, never quit on me," he said as he tried to control the release of his climax.

"I don't intend to," she promised as she sent them both over the edge.

***

Tonya looked around, satisfied with her progress. The Christmas tree would keep the office looking festive, even though they wouldn't be here.

The door opened, and a cold gust of wind blew in with Mrs. Sheffield. "Hi Tonya, dear. I brought you and Mr. Rhodes some homemade cookies."

"How sweet of you," Tonya said.

Mrs. Sheffield had the same radiant smile she always had, but it was nice to know there weren't any pressing financial worries behind the facade anymore.

"It was the least I could do."

Patrick came out of the office, reading a letter and without looking up, he asked, "Are you all packed up, honey?"

Mrs. Sheffield winked at Tonya, who blushed. When Patrick noticed the visitor, he smiled unashamed and warmly shook her hand.

"Hello, Mrs. Sheffield. It's great to see you."

"Hello, Mr. Rhodes. Are you making an honest woman out of Miss Corley here?"

Tonya grinned as she noticed Patrick's face flush red. In his defense, he had already asked her to marry him. Sort of. It had been his solution to working with someone he also wanted to undress.

"There's plenty of time for that, Mrs. Sheffield." Tonya hooked her arm under his to show her support.

"Just make sure you don't end up with a shotgun wedding, Mr. Rhodes."

"Yes, Ma'am," he said, his tone serious and respectful.

"Where are you two going?"

"Athens." Tonya grinned. They were leaving tomorrow to go on her biggest adventure yet.

"You two enjoy yourselves, my dears. And Merry Christmas." Mrs. Sheffield waved at them as she shuffled out of the office.

"Merry Christmas to you, too," Tonya and Patrick called after her.

As soon as the door shut, Patrick kissed her. "I can't wait to have you all to myself for two weeks," he said.

"Well, if you behave, I might stick around longer than that." Tonya grinned.

THE END

Please review my book...

It's hard to stand out (PUN not intended) as a romance author because there are many books published in the genre every day. If you liked "The Perfect Plan" and want to read more books like it, please help me by writing a quick review (one or two sentences would suffice).

Thank you!

Imperfectly *Perfect*

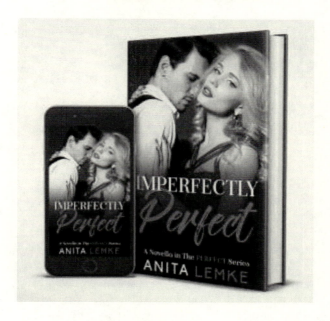

Daughters of wealthy parents don't get to pick their husbands... unless they do.

Download your free book here:
https://anitalemkeauthor.com/imperfectly-perfect/

Book 3: The *Perfect* Bet

Will she open her heart to her perfect husband and win the bet?

She's afraid to love anyone...
Solely focused on her career, ambitious Megan Rhodes never gets close to anyone—let alone a boyfriend. When her wealthy aunt offers her $200k to find the perfect guy, the goal is to draw Megan out of her shell. But Megan is determined to win the bet and start the ad agency she's always wanted to run without risking her heart.

... when the perfect husband captures her heart.
Megan convinces her teenage crush, outdoorsy Alex Whitmore, to become her husband for hire. Alex will do anything he can to help Megan win her bet—and he has own reasons. But when Megan's feelings for Alex become all too real, she must face her fears surrounding love while facing the genuine possibility of losing the bet and the perfect husband.

Manufactured by Amazon.ca
Acheson, AB